INFORMATION FOR BORROWERS
All books are stamped with date on which
they are due.
Each book kept overtime is subject to a fine
of five cents a day until its return.

MORTON PUBLIC LIBRARY
Morton, Illinois

THE
VIOLIN CASE
CASE

THE
VIOLIN CASE
CASE

Diantha Warfel

E. P. DUTTON   NEW YORK

Library of Congress Cataloging in Publication Data

Warfel, Diantha.   The violin case case.

SUMMARY: Bax's aspirations to join a symphony orchestra involve him with a beautiful and old violin which
is much desired by seemingly dangerous and elusive
strangers.

[1. Violins—Fiction.   2. Music—Fiction.
3. Mystery and detective stories]   I. Title.
PZ7.W23Vi   [Fic]   77-19049   ISBN: 0-525-41992-6

Published in the United States by E. P. Dutton, a Division
of Sequoia-Elsevier Publishing Company, Inc., New York
Published simultaneously in Canada by Clarke,
Irwin & Company Limited, Toronto and Vancouver

Editor: Ann Durell   Designer: Sallie Baldwin
Printed in the U.S.A.   First Edition
10 9 8 7 6 5 4 3 2 1

Dedicated to my Aunt Gertrude

CHAPTER

1

Bax rushed out of his music teacher's house and strapped his violin onto the handlebar of his bicycle.

He had just taken his last violin lesson until autumn. The long hot summer lay ahead of him—and in it lay his supersecret dream.

He wheeled away along the quiet street, with the supersecret dream spinning in his head. A clipping from the newspaper, folded in his pocket, told the facts. **Los Arboles Symphony Orchestra Being Formed.** How he yearned to play in it—a full-size symphony—doing the kind of music that sent him into orbit.

String auditions were scheduled for tomorrow. Could he qualify? Would they take a kid of twelve?

Hopes and doubts were rattling around in his head

1

as he signaled for a turn and cruised onto Spanish Trail Highway, heading for Cactus Acres Trailer Park.

One thing he had resolved for sure: He wasn't telling anyone a word about it till the auditions were over. If he made the grade, the world would know. But if he failed, nobody would know—not his best friend, Kip, not his parents—

But he hadn't figured on his Aunt Daphne.

As he slung open the glass door of the mobile home where he lived, there she sat. She perched on a hassock in the middle of the living room.

"Greetings, nephew Sebastian," said Aunt Daphne briskly. "I came to take your violin."

"But I need it!" His voice cracked with alarm.

Nobody ever knew what Aunt Daphne was going to do next. She had studied to be a concert violinist, but she got too busy getting married and divorced a few times to do much about a career.

"You do not need it," said Bax's mother. "School orchestra is disbanded. Your violin teacher is going away for the summer."

"But I do need it." He needed it at least tomorrow, for the auditions. Then, who could predict? Maybe all summer.

He sat rigidly in the leather easy chair. The leather felt cold against the back of his legs.

He knew he didn't look like much, in his torn Disneyland T-shirt and tattered cut-offs. But he clutched his battered violin case in his arms, ready to fight for it.

Aunt Daphne said, "I'm on my way to San Francisco, to visit friends who play a lot of chamber music."

2

So let her play a violin of her own, Bax thought angrily. Better still, let her stay home where she lived, in Munich, Germany.

His mother said, "I do not believe that you are going to practice all summer on your own, trying to develop a vibrato."

Vibrato was the shaking hand motion that made the tone big and beautiful. Would he ever master that?

Aunt Daphne was staring at him as if she could see into him. "You've got something on your mind, Sebastian. Out with it."

He took a deep breath. "I want to audition for the new Los Arboles Symphony Orchestra."

He slid back in the chair, his shoulders hunched, bracing for a put-down.

"You're dreaming," said his mother. "An adult symphony orchestra is no place for a child."

Anger bubbled up inside him. So he was only twelve—so he hadn't started the Growth Spurt like his tall friend Kip, or Susan Dodd. Still, he was no mere child. He had been taking violin lessons half his life. And anyhow, what was wrong with dreaming?

"Now, Helen," said Aunt Daphne. "I know these civic orchestras. They'll take anybody who can hold an instrument and stay awake."

Bax lurched forward, nearly dropping his violin in astonishment. Was she on his side? "You mean—you think I might make it?"

"Hop to it, Sebastian. With my blessings."

His heart soared. The blessings of an almost-concert-violinist ought to be a big boost.

3

His mother got up. "I'll see about supper."

"But Aunt Daphne." Bax leaned toward her anxiously. "I can't hop to it if I don't have a violin."

"I'm leaving you mine." She lowered her voice. "If you'll accept it."

"Why wouldn't I?" The troubled look on her face startled him. "Isn't it good?"

"It's very good." She glanced toward the kitchen area, beyond the dining counter, as if she didn't want his mother to hear. "Sebastian, are you brave?"

He recalled the time he crawled under Space 20's home, where there were black-widow spiders. Mrs. Johnson's poodle was under there, with its leash caught around one of the braces that held the house level. The poodle was nearly strangled, and Bax rescued it. Everybody in Cactus Acres called him brave then.

But the idea of auditioning for the symphony had him terrified. "Like about what?"

"Thieves. Somebody wants to steal that violin."

Bax stared at her. She was perfectly serious and obviously frightened. The fright seemed to grow and spread itself in the air around him, making his skin prickle. "But—why?"

"There is some mystery about it. I don't know what. I bought it in a musty little shop, in Schwabing District in Munich. I thought I saw somebody dodge away, around a corner, when I came out of the shop. And then—well, after what happened on shipboard, on my way to America, I'm afraid to carry it with me. That's why I want yours."

Bax's voice was almost a whisper. "What did happen?"

"I played the violin in the Ship's Concert. There was another passenger, a young man—he had been so attentive to me—really, I was sure I had fascinated him—"

Bax wriggled impatiently. He did not want her to get sidetracked onto the continuing soap opera of her love life. "But about the violin—"

"This *is* about the violin. You see, this young man accompanied me on the piano for the concert. But he was too nervous to play very well. Your mother plays infinitely better."

"I know, I know." His mother played piano infinitely better than a lot of people. But he didn't want Aunt Daphne getting sidetracked onto that either. "What was the man's name?"

"Emmet Hageman."

Bax leaped up in excitement. "That's the name of the conductor of the new symphony!" His mother looked across the dining counter at him, from the kitchen. He sat down again. "It's in the newspaper article announcing auditions."

"May he break an arm," Aunt Daphne said grimly. "Let me tell you what happened. After the concert that night—after I had gone to bed—in the dark—somebody broke into my stateroom and tried to get the violin."

"To steal it? You think it was this Emmet Hageman?"

"No, it was someone with a lot of hair. A mad mane of hair. I woke up and screamed and turned the light on, and that was all I saw. The person ran off."

Bax sat still, feeling a shudder of fear. The familiar sounds outside seemed oddly sharp. He heard his dog

5

Stub give a low gurgling growl, as if a cat had come too near his territory, and the clatter of the garbage can lid next door, as deaf old man Richter dumped something. "So why are you mad at Emmet Hageman?"

"Because he quit speaking to me. Gave me the brush-off. I am not used to such treatment."

Bax's mind churned. Could there be a connection between the concert, the attempted theft, and the brush-off? He wished he could get to the phone and consult with Kip. Kip preferred country and western to Bax's type of music, but he loved mystery and spy stuff.

But there was no time for consultation. He heard his father's car turning into the parking space out front.

"Aunt Daphne, do you suppose it is a real old master violin worth a fortune? I can take it to Mr. Rucci, out Rancho Road. He's a violinmaker who does appraisals. But—maybe it's stolen goods! Maybe the shopkeeper in Munich was a fence."

Aunt Daphne looked shocked. "Good heavens, don't suggest that to your father."

She was right. His father would certainly not take coolly to the possibility of his son and heir getting stuck with a hot fiddle.

He looked over at the violin, where it lay on top of the spinet piano in the alcove. The case was protected by a plain brown canvas cover.

What could it be like, that mysterious violin?

CHAPTER

At supper, Bax could hardly eat, waiting for Aunt Daphne to spring the news and to see how his father would take it.

She sprang it bluntly. "Charles, I am taking Sebastian's violin."

His father looked at her from under a frown. Then he transferred the look to Bax. "Is that all right with you, Bax?"

"It's all right."

"Six years of lessons, and you'll give up your instrument to a lady who already owns one?"

Aunt Daphne said, "I own four."

"And what you need is a fifth? Leaving this budding genius destitute?"

"I won't be destitute, Dad," said Bax hastily. "Aunt Daphne's leaving me the one she brought with her."

Here came the key question. His father demanded, "Why?"

Bax raised his eyes in appeal to Aunt Daphne. She was the one who had to answer that. But how could she answer it without giving away the secret of mystery that the violin carried with it?

Aunt Daphne stared at the ceiling, as if considering how to put this. Finally she stated, "I find it is not compatible with my temperament."

Bax relaxed. He knew this was the kind of answer his father would accept—and shrug off.

He remembered, for instance, the time his mother got the spinet piano. The mobile home salesman had been persuading them that this long narrow house on wheels would be the ideal residence for a loving close-knit family like the Barlows, and his mother said she could never bear to give up her grand piano. But then she went shopping, and came home and said joyfully, "I found a spinet that *speaks* to me."

Now his father just grunted and sliced more meat loaf. "You mean it doesn't speak to you. How much did you pay for it?"

Bax held his breath. Here was another hurdle. If she had paid an enormous amount, his father would say it was too fine an instrument for the budding genius to haul around on a bike.

"Sixteen hundred German marks."

Bax watched his father's face, knowing he was doing a lightning conversion at international exchange

8

rates. His father nodded coolly. "You have the bill of sale, for insurance purposes?"

"Oh yes. That is, I'm sure I have. Somewhere in my luggage. I'll look for it."

"And you will be playing the violin for us after supper?"

"I was hoping you'd ask."

Bax grinned. Aunt Daphne couldn't tell when his father was putting her on.

He gulped his food faster. He was perched uncomfortably on the thickest volume of his *Encyclopedia for Strings,* to bring his chair seat up to the level of the three long-legged stools the others were sitting on at the dining counter.

Finally they polished off banana pudding. "May I open the case? Now? Please?"

"Open," said Aunt Daphne grandly. "And just you wait till you see that case. It will knock your eye out."

She wasn't kidding. Bax unzipped the canvas cover and laid it back and said, "Wow."

The violin case was made of soft suede leather in a beige color. It had intricate gold patterns traced all around the edges.

He ran his finger over the delicate suede. It was gorgeous. The very idea of having a case like that to carry to audition gave him a surge of confidence.

His father peered over Bax's head and said, "Remarkable." That, from him, amounted to *supercolossal* from anyone else.

His mother stopped loading the dishwasher long enough to come take a look. "But it is much too valu-

9

able a case for you to wheel around town strapped to your handlebar, Basty."

His mother still used his old nickname, and he let her. At school, it was different. His friend Kip had invented *Bax*, and he and Kip knocked a few heads until they made the change stick.

He cried, "Oh, I'll be careful."

"And you told me the hinges on your case are tearing loose. You can't expect your Aunt Daphne to travel around with that."

Bax groaned. She was right. He could just imagine the hinges finally giving out while Aunt Daphne charged up a ramp to board an airplane. Bows and strings and rosin cake and shoulder pad would spew all over the place, along with his violin.

He thought fast. "She can take this brown canvas cover and put it over my pasteboard case. That will hold it together."

"But this one—"

"—needs a cover too. You can *make* one, Mother! You have all that denim left that you bought on sale to make my music bag—"

"Basty, I don't have a zipper long enough for that. And I can't buy one in time, if you're going to audition tomorrow."

If he was going? He was, he was.

"You have some hammer-on snaps, don't you? If you'll sew the cover, I'll hammer them on."

That, he knew, would get her. She was always for family togetherness and cooperative projects.

She smiled at him brightly. "I'm glad you thought

of it. I'll sew a cover for you the first thing tomorrow morning."

Bax looked the case over carefully. The bottom was of darker leather than the top, and not so finely patterned. Apparently the maker had been less painstaking about the part that didn't show so often. But the inside was handsome. The violin lay snuggled in royal purple velvet.

He pointed to a pearly decoration on the tailpiece of the violin. "Look, the Boy Scout emblem."

"That is a fleur-de-lis." Aunt Daphne snapped the bow out from its place in the lid.

"What's a fleur-de-lis?"

"Look it up in the dictionary."

It vaguely rang a bell in his mind. Hadn't some old violinmaker, a disciple of the famous Antonio Stradivari, used something that looked like that as his trademark?

Bax's mother settled herself on the piano stool, saying, "Beethoven?"

He expected that. These two sisters were bears for playing music by Beethoven. And Bach—Johann Sebastian Bach, the man he was named for.

Aunt Daphne tuned her strings. "And some Bach, if we have time."

Bax's father said loud and clear, "There will be no time for Bach," and he sounded as if that suited him fine. "Not if Daphne is going to make that plane to Los Angeles and make connection there to San Francisco tonight." He sat down on the sofa.

Bax flopped beside him. The louvers of the window

were open. He could hear soft evening noises. Traffic hummed, out on Spanish Trail Highway. Voices murmured from Space 39, where the people always barbecued and ate outside.

His mother brought her hands down on a full chord on the piano, and Aunt Daphne launched into a rich round phrase of music on the violin. Bax folded his hands over his stomach blissfully and closed his eyes. The music reached a loud high climax, and suddenly dropped to a faint soft sigh.

Bax heard a noise outside. "Yip, yip." His dog, Stub, had started barking.

He sat up straight. If Stub went into one of his barking fits, he'd ruin the music.

"Relax," whispered his father.

"But now he's growling."

"Cat around nearby."

"I don't think that's his cat growl." He listened intently. The growl rumbled, mean, threatening. Bax felt the skin across his throat tighten. "That's his people growl!"

"Mr. Richter strolling out for a newspaper."

"No." Stub would never growl that way at someone he knew. Bax got up. Prowling out there, in the twilight, could be some evil stranger.

CHAPTER

Bax tiptoed past the performers. He slipped out through the dark kitchen, into the service area, and sidled carefully past washing machine and dryer and water heater without bumping into anything.

Quietly he opened the back door—and listened.

Did he hear a slight scrape? Was that a sound like feet on the gravelly desert crust—out beyond the pole that carried the wiring?

He strained his ears. But the music was swelling to a climax again. His mother was pounding full chords of the accompaniment with all her power.

He stepped out carefully, trying to tread lightly on the wooden stair unit that his father had built. It had a tendency to creak.

Suddenly the piano stopped. The violin sustained a long high tone. Bax heard a scrape, like a footstep. Something was moving, up toward the front.

Tiptoeing, holding his breath, Bax moved toward the sound.

The air was luminous, gentle, just in the in-between twilight stage where a person could not see precisely. Distances were hard to judge. The western sky was still a smolder of orange.

Stub was underneath the mobile home, by the wheels. The growl burst into a yip.

Bax darted forward. Somebody spurted away!

Bax ran. But the fugitive scooted out through the gate and dove behind the oleanders that screened old man Richter's carport. He glimpsed only one thing for sure—bushy hair, sticking out in all directions. "A mad mane of hair," his aunt had said.

He tried to follow, but it was no use. The person disappeared behind a toolshed. He heard cracklings of a plunge through the tamarack barrier that fenced the trailer park. Whoever it was, was off and running through the desert mesquite.

Bax stood in the roadway, frustrated. Quivering with disappointment, he listened for a minute to the distant rattle of the freight train to Los Angeles and smelled the familiar pungency of sparerib drippings from Space 39's barbecue.

He could ask old man Richter if he had seen the person run across his property. But that would have to wait till tomorrow. It took time to ask old man Richter anything. He was deaf, and you had to write your questions on a slate.

Stub wriggled out from beneath the mobile home. Bax patted him. "Good dog, good dog."

Glumly Bax trudged back in.

His father asked, "Did you trap the Mafia?"

"They got away. He, or she, or it, or whoever it was."

"Cat."

Bax silently shook his head. That was no cat, the size of a man, with a head of bushy hair.

"Better pack up, Daphne," his father ordered. "We have to move if we're going to get you on that plane."

Bax zipped the canvas cover over his old violin case for her.

"The tone of that violin is great," he said. "That should help me make a good showing at the audition."

"That, plus a decent vibrato," said Aunt Daphne. "How is your vibrato?"

"Nowhere. I haven't got one. I plant the fingers of my left hand on the string and try to shake—"

"No, no, don't shake. Rock, Sebastian. Like a tiny rocking chair. Roll back and forth on the finger end."

He repeated, "Rock and roll." Excitement was welling up inside him. Could he really do it?

His father called, "Coming to the airport with us?"

"No. I want to try out my new violin."

When his parents and aunt had left, the silence felt strange. He could hear the monotonous chirp of a cricket, and a soft *slurp-slurp* as Stub drank from his water bowl.

A puff of breeze drifted in through the window, carrying the lingering odor of barbecue from Space 39. The smell sent a shiver through him as he remembered

15

the mysterious prowler out there in the dark. He locked the door.

Now to try the fabulous violin—and to try to play it with vibrato. He fitted the violin beneath his chin, lifted the bow, and applied what Aunt Daphne had suggested—to rock and roll upon the finger end.

Wonder of wonders, it began to work. He played his new recital piece, and the tone vibrated full and round, all the way through to the final note, long . . . fading . . . faint . . . gone.

And he heard something again, outside. Stub was growling again. His scalp prickled. Someone must be out there in the dark—again.

He put the violin and bow in the case with trembling hands. He kept listening, hearing that eternal cricket. Where would the violin be safe? Nowhere, really. But he slid it under the sofa, far back underneath.

With thudding heart, he crossed the room stealthily and stood by the window of the alcove. Stub had stopped growling. Was the prowler gone? No, there was a sound—a scraping sound—just below the window. And there was a rubbing noise too, as if a person might be leaning against the house, rubbing against the siding.

Bax crept to the back exit and then made a rush. He jumped down the stairs and swung toward the front. He took huge steps—running—veering around the corner of the projecting alcove.

And he slammed right into somebody leaning there. Both of them fell to the ground in the darkness, grappling.

16

CHAPTER

They rolled on the gritty gravel. Bax was on top, his opponent's arms around him. He pushed outward with his elbows, struggling to free himself. The opponent let go with one arm, and Bax was flung backward, banging his shoulder against a concrete supporting block. The opponent rolled to one side, and Bax lunged, grabbing him. He pinned him to the ground, face down.

"Who are you?" Bax gasped. "What do you want?"

"It's me—Kip," answered a muffled voice. "I'm friend. Not foe."

"Kip!" Bax let go.

As fear subsided, anger welled up. All this buildup, all the suspicion and the mustering of courage—had it all been just for a dumb prank? "What's the idea, Kip, creeping around here like a sneak? Where is your hair this time?"

"On my head." Kip sat up, brushing at his face. "What do you mean, *this time?*"

Bax stared at him. He looked ghostly in the darkness. "You mean you weren't here before? Earlier this evening?"

"Not me. I was over at school. They're getting summer crafts organized. I have witnesses."

Bax could feel anger oozing away and fear seeping back in again. "But somebody was here, earlier. Somebody came prowling around, and Stub growled at him."

"He growled at me too, till I told him to cool it. He knew my voice."

Bax got slowly to his feet. "But why are you sneaking around like this?"

"I was being polite. I didn't want to ring the doorbell and interrupt while your aunt was playing. I don't go much for that kind of music, but she sure sounds good."

"She ought to. She studied for a concert career." He stuck out a hand to help Kip up.

Kip asked, "Is this what the other prowler did—just hang around like this, listening?"

"But he wasn't just being polite. He wants the violin."

"What violin?"

"Come on in and I'll tell you about it."

"Lure me with food." Kip's biggest hobby was eating, since he had started growing so tall.

"Banana pudding?"

18

"It's a deal."

Bax led the way up the wooden stairs. At the top he suddenly stopped. "Say, Kip—how did you know my aunt was here?"

"Simple deduction. I hear fine violin playing. I know you have an aunt who is a fine violinist. I say to myself that has got to be the aunt."

Bax lifted his chin high. Pride spread a smile across his face as he opened the door and marched in. "She was here earlier, but she's not here now. That wasn't my aunt who was playing."

"Then who was it?"

"Me."

"You?" Kip crossed the kitchen and settled on a stool at the dining counter. "I know you're pretty good, Bax. I mean, you're first chair in the first violins of the school orchestra. But I'd have sworn that was your aunt. What happened?"

Bax rinsed his hands at the sink and rubbed water on his dusty face. He knew there was no point in giving Kip a lecture on vibrato. One day when Kip was visiting and a storm put the electricity out, Kip sat and read by candlelight in Bax's *Encyclopedia for Strings*—and said afterward that it told him more about violins than he cared to know.

"I was playing on that special violin." Bax searched in the refrigerator. "Ah, here is your banana pudding, sir. I trust it will meet with your approval."

"Thank you, waiter. I will give it my attention. What violin?"

"The one the prowler wants. My aunt just bought

it recently." Bax leaned across the counter. "There is something terribly mysterious about that violin, Kip. That's why she left it here with me. She was afraid to go on carrying it around herself. Somebody tried to steal it from her on the ship coming over!"

"Steal it? It must be valuable. Maybe it's a—there was a famous name in your book. Strad, shmad—"

"Stradivarius. That was how he put his name on the violin labels."

"I remember. Antonio Stradivari. Cremona, Italy. Seventeen hundred and something. Greatest violinmaker in history. Maybe that's what you've got."

Bax frowned. "I don't think so. It's a good instrument, all right, but if it was as wonderful as a Strad, Aunt Daphne would have known right away. No, there's something else, some special reason why somebody is after it."

"Maybe it has a concealed compartment. Maybe it's loaded with contraband. Diamonds. Cash."

"I don't see how there could be anything concealed in a violin. Not without wrecking the tone."

Kip scraped up the last of the pudding. "Where is it?"

Bax inquired solemnly, "First tell me, how was the pudding, sir? Did you find it satisfactory?"

"The pudding was entirely satisfactory, waiter. You may add the charge to my bill."

"Yes, sir. Glad to, sir. That brings your bill to eight hundred and forty-seven dollars."

"See my lawyer. Where's that violin?" Kip swung around toward the living room. "I don't see any violin."

Bax dove down on his stomach in front of the sofa. He clawed beneath it to drag out the violin case. "Here it is."

Kip nodded. "Of course. Sure. That's where normal people always stash violins. Under sofas."

"I hid it for safekeeping when I heard you out there, Kip. I thought it was the same prowler that was here when my mother and aunt were playing. I tracked him and saw that he had a head of bushy hair—just like the thief who broke into my aunt's stateroom."

"Let me see the violin."

"First observe case," said Bax. "Fine leather, gold decorations—"

Kip turned it over. "Finer on top than on bottom. Very unusual. Make a note of that, Watson."

"Noted, Sherlock. Now look at the inside." Bax opened the case. "Purple velvet. Royal purple."

Kip pointed to the fleur-de-lis on the tailpiece of the violin and came out with the name of the old master violinmaker that Bax had been trying to think of. "Del Fiore. He's in your encyclopedia. Say, Bax, do you suppose it is a real Del Fiore?"

"Maybe. It could be. You know, it's going to be some responsibility, carrying this around all summer."

Kip shrugged. "But where's to carry? School orchestra is out. Your teacher's gone. Just leave it here, safe under the sofa."

"I hope I'm going to be taking it to rehearsals, Kip." Here it came again—confession of his cherished ambition. "I'm going to audition for the new Los Arboles Symphony Orchestra."

21

Kip stared at him. And then he nodded. "If you play like you played tonight, you just might make it."

Bax bowed gratefully, bending from the waist. "I truly thank you for your confidence."

"But if you pedal around town with that violin case right out in plain sight, you're asking for trouble."

"I know. That's why I got my mother to promise to sew a cover for it, first thing tomorrow."

"That should help," said Kip. "But even if it's covered, the person who wants it will find out you have it."

"My aunt is carrying her old brown cover. He'll think she took the violin away with her."

"He may think so now. But he'll find out different. And then if he comes around the symphony and sees that little decoration—"

"Fleur-de-lis."

"—he'll know."

Bax shuddered. Kip was right.

"He'll know," Bax agreed fearfully. "And then— he'll make his move, whatever that may be."

It was more than just a responsibility, having that violin. It was a risk. Anything might happen.

CHAPTER

Kip took off on his bicycle just before Bax's parents came in.

His mother took a look around the room and demanded, "Who had banana pudding?"

"Kip."

"The dish is still on the counter."

"Sorry about that." Bax took the dish to the kitchen sink. He washed it with a lot of splashing and extra motion, to demonstrate how wonderfully clean he was getting it. But he couldn't help smiling to himself. Other people's kids were out getting busted for pushing drugs, while his mother could get worked up over a dish left on the counter.

His father settled in the easy chair. "I am told that you are hoping to audition for the symphony."

"Not just hoping—I'm planning. Auditions will be held tomorrow afternoon, in the Desert Star Hotel showroom."

"If they are held at all."

Bax asked in alarm, "Why wouldn't they be?"

"We saw the conductor at the airport."

"What does he look like?" Bax inquired eagerly. Like a mean monster who would say, "No kids in my orchestra"? Or like a nice guy who would say, "Welcome, lad"?

His mother said, "Quite attractive, in a bony way. I'm glad for Daphne. I do believe he really likes her."

"Aunt Daphne? But he gave her the brush-off."

His father said, "It may have changed to the brush-on. He left town on the same plane with her."

"Left town!" Weren't there going to be any auditions? Was the whole orchestra project going to fall through?

Bax's mind whirled, then halted at a decision. "I'm going to the Desert Star tomorrow anyhow. Maybe he's having somebody else run the auditions, and he'll just come back to conduct the rehearsals."

But that, he knew, didn't make much sense. A conductor would want to select his musicians personally. He wouldn't go flying out of town without some urgent reason. Bax couldn't help worrying. Aunt Daphne had his violin with her, not the mysterious one in the fancy case—but she had her own brown canvas cover on it. If Mr. Hageman thought she had *the* violin, and if he was the person who wanted it, what might he do to her to get it?

And then he would find out it was the wrong one.

Bax had his name and his junior high school instrument locker number stenciled inside the case lid. It would not take long for Mr. Hageman to figure out who had the violin he was after. And then he would come for Bax.

He picked up the fine violin case and cradled it in his arms, *handle with care*, to carry it back to his room. The mobile home was built like a railroad car, long and narrow. Bax's small room was at the far end.

He fell asleep that night worrying. He was still worrying the next morning, while he practiced his audition piece.

His mother came back to his room and thrust the new blue-denim case cover in through the door. "I've sewed the seams, Basty. It's ready for the hammer-on snaps."

"Hey, thanks."

He gathered up cover, card of snaps, and hammer, and hurried out to the ornamental boulder beside Stub's doghouse.

He found out that it was a harder job than he had expected. Jobs he volunteered for often turned out that way. He measured carefully. Placed Ring A where it should meet Teeth B. Hit too hard with the hammer, mashing Teeth. When he hit too light on the next try, Ring did not take hold.

Sun beat on his back. He could hear the roaring and scraping of heavy road equipment out on the highway. They were ditching for storm drains out there. Yesterday he had seen huge pipes lined up along the road, big enough for him almost to stand in.

He finally finished the last snap and heard a rasping harsh voice say, "Working hard there, sonny?"

He jumped up. Old man Richter, next door, was looking at him over the hedge.

Here was his chance to ask about last night's prowler—to have proof that it was a person, not an outsize science fiction cat.

Mr. Richter was holding out an old-fashioned slate, and a piece of chalk. Bax wrote on it, *Did you see somebody—running—last night—about suppertime?*

Mr. Richter nodded his white head. "The fellow cut right past my toolshed. Out into the desert."

Bax erased. Chalk dust stuck to his damp hand. He wrote, *What sort of fellow? Could you see his face?*

"No. Just noticed hair. Bushy lot of hair."

His mother called, "Basty, lunch."

He scribbled *Thanks* and gathered up his materials. There really had been a prowler. He had a witness.

He knew he was too excited to eat, but he had to make a pretense of it, or his mother would expect him to faint. After lunch, he dressed neatly, fastened the violin to the handlebar of his bike, and set off to his fate.

Bax seldom went down to the long avenue of tall resort hotels, the chief industry of Los Arboles. He had never gone there on his bike alone. It was an adventure into new territory.

Arriving at the Desert Star, he chained his bike to a newspaper rack at the ornately decorated entrance. Inside, he found the large lobby crowded and noisy. Lights winked from elaborate chandeliers. Bright murals on the walls depicted historical events of the Spanish conquest of the Southwest.

He elbowed his way among the tourists, toward the

door of the showroom. SYMPHONY AUDITIONS, STRINGS ONLY, said a penciled sign. This was it.

He pushed open the door and stepped inside. It was dark and quiet. He blinked until his eyes got used to the gloom. Gradually he made out the shape of the room, a semicircle of broad terraces on which stood the tables and chairs for the supper show customers. The stage thrust out in a great half circle, with a grand piano on it. A work light stood by the piano, bare and glaring.

Two men were sitting at one of the tables, down in front of the stage. One of them was a burly bald person with an unlighted cigar in his mouth. Bax recognized him from newspaper pictures. It was Mr. Hector Bolden, owner of this hotel and president of the new Symphony Association.

Bax's hand clutched the violin case handle tighter. Was Mr. Bolden going to have a say as to who passed audition and who didn't? He looked like the kind who would bellow "No kids" before anybody Bax's age could even unpack.

The other man had to be Emmet Hageman. Bax squinted, trying to study him in the gloom. He was thin, with a long face. Light glinted on dark-rimmed glasses. Lank blond hair was combed back.

So he had not gone on to San Francisco with Aunt Daphne. He must have turned right around in Los Angeles and come back. Why had he gone at all?

Bax stared so hard that some ESP seemed to get through—Mr. Hageman suddenly looked up toward the door and spotted him.

"You have come to audition?" Mr. Hageman's

words tumbled out fast, as if he had a lot of things to think about all at the same time.

Bax heard Mr. Bolden growl, "Awfully young, isn't he?"

He tensed. Did they have an age limit? Was he below it?

Mr. Hageman said, "Some start young." He ordered Bax, "Wait over by that cello. Now, Mr. Fitting."

The call for Mr. Fitting was directed toward the stage.

Bax looked nervously around, and saw a woman sitting at one of the tables to his right. On the floor beside her, he could make out the bulk of a cello lying on its side.

He shuffled toward her and slid into a chair.

On the stage, a short pale man with a violin, doubtless Mr. Fitting, came forward. Behind him came a large lady with a square stern face. Bax knew her. She was Mrs. Mansifer, who played organ at church when his mother couldn't make it. Mrs. Mansifer was bad news. When she accompanied a soloist, she charged into a tempo of her own choosing, and kept it up relentlessly, even if the soloist couldn't go that fast.

Mr. Fitting put his violin under his chin and launched into an intricate passage of music without even glancing at Mrs. Mansifer.

The woman beside Bax groaned. "Listen to the competition."

He was feeling sicker with every tone that poured forth from the performer onstage, smooth and expert. The man seemed as calm as if this were just routine, as if he played a violin in a showroom big enough to seat five hundred people every day. He probably did. Bax had read newspaper articles about how the symphony expected its major membership to come from hotel orchestras, "skilled performers of contemporary jazz who will be glad to get their teeth into the classics for a change."

"He's no competition for you," Bax whispered back. "You're a cello. But I'm a violin."

"You should be a viola," said the woman. "Orchestras are always so hard up for violas, you probably wouldn't even have to audition."

The only viola player Bax knew very well was Susan Dodd at school. He was glad she wasn't around. She was so much taller than he was, she made him uncomfortable.

The woman whispered, "You go next."

A chill swept him. "But you were here before I was."

"I haven't played in years. I'm as nervous as I was at my first recital. You go next!"

CHAPTER

The music sparkled on, while Bax felt smaller and more uncomfortable by the minute. The air of the room was chilly and smelled of stale smoke. Other people were coming in. There was a small man with an enormous bass viol, then two large women with violins, and a bearded black man with a cello. Bax had seen him before, at a recital at the university.

The violinist onstage ended his piece with a flourish, half a measure ahead of Mrs. Mansifer.

Bax heard Mr. Hageman say, "Thank you, Mr. Fitting. Leave your address and phone number with the secretary here," indicating a young man sitting at a table behind him.

Mrs. Mansifer, on the piano bench, turned, looking angry, as if she felt mistreated by Mr. Fitting gaining half a measure on her. "Mr. Hageman, aren't you forgetting the sight reading?"

Sight reading! Instant ice seemed to form around Bax's heart. For a sight-reading test, they stuck a completely unknown piece of music in front of you and said, "Play this." And you had to play it right off. It was sink or swim.

Mr. Hageman said, "In this candidate's case, I feel it is not necessary. Next audition!"

The cello lady beside him said, "That's you."

Clumsily, Bax hobbled to the stage and put his violin case up on it, while he stood down on floor level. He started unsnapping the snaps, and naturally the ones on which he had hammered too hard stuck.

Mrs. Mansifer loomed above him. "Well, hand me your music, child," she said impatiently.

Child. He felt his face turning red all the way down under his ears, as he handed her the music of the piano accompaniment. He opened the violin case as craftily as possible. He did not want Mr. Hageman to see it and recognize that it was the one that belonged to his aunt. It seemed like an age, with all eyes on him, until he finally got the violin out, shoulder pad on, bow tightened. He stumbled up the steps, onto the stage.

Mrs. Mansifer thumped an A on the piano, for him to tune. Then she thumped a chord to go with the A, and then a lot of rippling arpeggios up and down the piano to go with the chord. Bax could hardly hear his own strings as he tried to tune them.

Suddenly she broke off her warm-up. "Why, I

know you," she cried. "You're the little Barlow boy."

Little boy was a low blow. But in a way it gave him hope. Maybe knowing him would make her feel more kindly. She might try to help him make a good impression.

She was beaming toward Mr. Hageman. "I know this boy's mother, an excellent pianist. And his aunt. His aunt is a superb violinist. She studied with—"

Bax panicked. He must not let Mrs. Mansifer broadcast who his aunt was. If Mr. Hageman was brushing her off, he wouldn't want her relative in his orchestra. He said loudly, "I've taken lessons since I was six."

Mrs. Mansifer gave him a look of annoyance and slammed into the accompaniment without even looking to see whether Bax was ready. He wasn't. He plunged into the music and played in a kind of foggy frenzy, hardly hearing himself. Only the reflexes developed through years of practicing pulled him through.

Mrs. Mansifer won the race this time. She crashed the final chord a full measure ahead of Bax.

He saw Mr. Bolden mutter something to Mr. Hageman. What could it be? The *out* signal? Mr. Bolden, he had read, was putting a lot of money into this venture. Mr. Hageman would have to be paid, union members would get the scale wage, music must be bought. Was he saying, "No small fry"?

Mr. Hageman hurled out, "Sight reading."

Mrs. Mansifer went to the rear of the stage and brought out a stand with some music on it. She put it in front of Bax and said harshly, "This is Beethoven," as if that was going to be his downfall and serve him right.

32

He stared at the music. "L. van Beethoven, Overture to *Coriolanus*. Violino I." This was the real thing.
It started with a long lone loud middle C, for a full
count of eight. What was this, anyhow? Anybody could
play middle C and count eight.

But Mr. Hageman called, "Start at measure fifteen."

Bax counted cautiously. Measure fifteen was the
beginning of a melody, written in eighth notes, to be
played softly. It didn't look too hard. He shouldered the
violin, which felt as if it weighed twenty pounds. Tap-
ping time with his foot, he attacked the music.

The next thing he knew was the sound of Mr.
Hageman's voice. "I *said*, that will be *enough*."

Laughter rippled from the people waiting their
turn. Embarrassment made his insides quiver.

Mr. Hageman said, "Give your name, address, and
phone number to the secretary. You will be notified of
the result of your audition. Next!"

The woman at the table got up and started down
the aisle with her cello.

Bax turned too fast and knocked the music stand
over. Overture to *Coriolanus* fell at Mrs. Mansifer's
feet. He scrambled to collect the music from the floor.

Mr. Bolden bellowed, "Clear the stage. We're
wasting time."

Bax put the violin under his arm. He snatched up
the case, but dropped the denim cover. He knelt and
picked it up, and then nearly tangled with the cello as
he went down the stairs while the woman was coming
up.

He hurried past Mr. Hageman and Mr. Bolden, to the secretary's table. There everything tumbled onto the table—the violin, the case, the cover, all separately.

Mr. Bolden and Mr. Hageman both swung around and stared.

Mr. Bolden demanded, "Where did you get that violin?"

Mr. Hageman demanded, "Where did you get that case?"

CHAPTER

It was one of those moments when time seems to stand still.

The woman onstage was tuning the strings of her cello. Mrs. Mansifer was rendering ripples on the piano. Mr. Hageman and Mr. Bolden were gazing at Bax as if he were a criminal caught in the act. But what act?

Bax said feebly, "They belong to my aunt."

Mr. Hageman took off his glasses. His eyes were intensely blue. "But she's gone. She took her violin with her."

Mr. Bolden looked at Mr. Hageman sharply. "How do you know?"

"I flew to Los Angeles with her last night." Mr. Hageman glanced at Bax and looked uncomfortable. "I had to go there—on business."

Some funny business, Bax thought darkly. "That was my violin she had with her. She loaned me this one for the summer."

Mr. Bolden reached out his pudgy hand. Very delicately he rubbed his finger across the little mother-of-pearl fleur-de-lis. "Why?"

Did Mr. Hageman's face turn red? The light was so eerie in this dim showroom, Bax could not be sure.

How much should he tell? He hedged, saying, "She likes mine better."

Mr. Bolden demanded, "Where did she get this one?"

"She bought it in Europe."

"And she took yours—in preference to this one?" Mr. Bolden narrowed his eyes at Bax as if he didn't believe a word he said.

Bax thought fast, and then said, "Mine's not so fancy. She thought it would be safer—for traveling with."

Mrs. Mansifer quit warming up at the piano. The room was silent. Mr. Bolden dropped his voice low. "She is right to be so cautious. This may be—an extremely—valuable—violin."

An idea exploded in Bax's head. Could Mr. Bolden have been last night's prowler? He was bald—but he could have worn a wig. He might even have been in touch with the other prowler, the one on shipboard. There might be a whole network of people after the violin.

Mr. Hageman reached out and clutched at the edge of the open case. Bax could see his knuckles white

36

against the deep purple of the velvet. "Bring it with you to rehearsals."

To rehearsals! Bax felt skyrockets go off in his mind. "You mean—I'm in? I qualify for the symphony?"

Mr. Hageman nodded brusquely. He repeated, "Bring that violin with you to rehearsals."

He was in! Skyrockets and firecrackers! He could hardly wait to break the news to Kip.

He felt like a different person now, striding out through the crowded lobby, confidently bumping people to move them out of his way.

The sunlight glared blindingly when he came out of the hotel. With violin strapped on handlebar, he pedaled briskly down the thoroughfare—then past small businesses and along used-car row. The sun was hot on his back, but the breeze was cool against his face, as there were still some strings of snow draped on distant Paiute Peak.

Oleanders bloomed everywhere, white, pink, red. They seemed extra brilliant today. Olive trees looked dusty, a soft, friendly shade of green.

He signaled for a right turn past a sprawling apartment complex. There was a red car behind him. The red car turned too.

A creepy feeling began to inch up the back of his neck. He watched in the little round mirror attached to his handlebar. How long had the red car been following him?

He made some fast calculations about his route. Kip's home was in a hilly residential area. Bax knew a way through narrow streets that avoided the major ups and downs. It was longer than the main route, but for a bicycle rider it was usually worth the extra time; it saved so much on breath and muscle.

He had intended to pump ahead on the harder shorter route today. But now he changed his mind. If he took the flat narrow way, he would probably succeed in losing that car, as cars generally took the main road.

He wove carefully over to the left turn lane, signaled, turned.

The red car turned left too, directly behind him.

In the mirror, he tried to make out what kind of person was driving. Tousled brown hair hung straight to the shoulders. Huge, heavily rimmed spectacles obscured the eyes.

Fear powered his legs to go as fast as he could, but the car kept on with a steady deliberate pace.

Then he slowed down, barely crawling. That should force the car to pass. But the car crawled too.

With his heart thumping, he wheeled on into Kip's part of town. Here, large houses were set in emerald green lawns that took a lot of loving care and a lot of water. He wobbled along the winding way toward Kip's place. The red car was still behind him.

Would it dare to follow him up Kip's graveled drive?

He turned in.

The car turned in too! Bax felt his heart skip beats.

He parked at Kip's kitchen door and tore wildly at the straps holding the violin. He was going to shield that violin with his body, if need be.

The red car eased to a stop—right by the bike. A raspy noise sounded as the driver set the hand brake.

The driver jumped out.

Clutching the violin, Bax flattened himself against the side of the house.

CHAPTER

The driver, in plaid shirt, blue jeans, boots, stomped right past Bax and into Kip's kitchen. Bax bolted in too.

Kip was at the sink, mixing red fruit drink. Country music pounded from the transistor radio on the counter.

Bax gasped, "This person—he followed me—"

"Hi, Bax," Kip yelled cheerfully above the music. "Hi, Angela May. You want to use the phone?"

Bax gasped. It was a teenage girl. She grabbed for the phone that hung on the wall. "I want to use the phone, and a lot of strong language, and a ball bat," she growled, punching digits. "On George. George?"

Bax stood there while Angela May gave George a piece of her mind. "George, those brakes went out on me again. You get right over to our place with all your tools, or Mother's going to make me sell the car."

She slammed the phone down and marched out.

Bax sank weakly onto a bench of the breakfast nook, laying the violin on the table. "She followed me, no matter how slow I went, even though I took the long slow route."

Kip poured a glass of fruit drink and set it in front of Bax. "Angela May lives across the street. Her brakes are bad. Her boyfriend promised to fix them."

Bax sputtered, shouting above the music. "But why follow me? Why come here?"

"She wasn't following you. You just happened to be ahead of her. She uses our phone when she doesn't want her mother to hear."

Bax took a long swig from his glass. The fear ebbed, subsided, finally drained all away. In its place, jubilation surged. "Hey, guess what?"

Kip turned the music down to a mild roar and studied Bax's face. "You're in the orchestra! You made it."

"How can you tell?"

"You're grinning like six birthdays and Christmas. I can see the headlines now: **Mystery Violin Played by Youngest Member of Symphony.**"

Bax grinned even wider. "Waiter, do you have peanut butter on the menu today?"

"Yes, indeed, sir," said Kip. "Peanut butter is one of our more popular items. May I create a sandwich for you, sir?"

"You sure may." He settled back, thinking over the events of the afternoon. "You know what, Kip? I think the symphony conductor is some kind of a nut."

"What kind of a nut? Tell me."

41

"His name is Emmet Hageman. He came over from Europe on the same ship as my Aunt Daphne."

"Aha! He tried to steal the violin."

"No, he wasn't the one. He has straight floppy hair. But he acts funny. First he acted as if he was really crazy about my aunt—"

"Is that nutty?"

"Oh no, she always has men falling in love with her. But he suddenly stopped speaking to her."

"Very strange. Do you care for lettuce on your sandwich, sir?"

"Just a little lettuce, waiter. But last night he flew from here to Los Angeles with her. And he flew right back."

Kip stopped tearing lettuce leaves and looked up. "With your aunt?"

"Without."

"Do you think he disposed of her? What's his motive?"

"Whatever he's up to, I'm sure his motives have something to do with the violin."

"Your sandwich, sir." Kip slapped the plate onto the table. "Did he notice that you had it, this afternoon?"

"Notice! He about had a fit. You never saw anybody so surprised. And do you know who took a mighty weird interest too? Mr. Bolden."

"Mr. Bolden? Bolden, Shmolden—" Kip sat on the table, swinging his legs. "Oh, him."

"What do you mean, 'oh, him'? Do you know about him?"

"I've read about him."

"I should have known."

"I read a Sunday feature. On Mr. Hector Bolden. He owns the Desert Star Hotel. He's a big culture vulture. Collects paintings, and porcelain, and harpsichords—"

Bax coughed on a bite, trying to picture dumpy Mr. Bolden, cigar in face, seated sedately before the keyboard of a harpsichord and tinkling delicate tunes. Did he collect violins, too? Old master violins? Del Fiores? "You know, Kip, I didn't like the way he looked at the violin."

"How?"

"As if he wanted to eat it."

"He can afford steak."

"Not eat with teeth. More like just—greed."

Kip swung his feet. The refrigerator hummed.

Kip said, "Bax, I am having an idea I don't think you will like."

Bax hunched his shoulders. "What idea?"

"Maybe they only let you into the orchestra so they can keep tabs on the violin."

"You mean maybe I'm not good enough? I'm just in on tolerance? But last night you thought I was playing so terrific, you thought I was my aunt."

"But I am not your average everyday symphony conductor," Kip pointed out.

Feeling punctured, Bax sagged back against the yellow vinyl of the bench. "You sure know how to rain on a guy's parade."

"I could be wrong."

"You bet you could. You don't even know how a symphony orchestra is supposed to sound."

"I have a rough idea."

"Very rough. Hey, Kip—come to rehearsal. It's in the Arroyo High School auditorium, Friday."

"Me come? What for?"

Excited, Bax leaned forward. "To case the joint. Search for clues. Observe suspects. We've got a mystery on our hands, man. Don't you see?"

Kip jumped down from the table. "I'll do it."

"Great." Bax dusted crumbs from his fingers. "That was an excellent sandwich, waiter. Put it on my bill."

Kip frowned. "Your bill is well over a thousand dollars, sir. I'm afraid we can't extend you any more credit."

Bax patted the violin case lovingly. "Suppose I offer to put this valuable instrument up for collateral."

"Oh, in that case, your credit is unlimited."

CHAPTER

It was the afternoon of the first rehearsal. The Arroyo High School auditorium was dim and cool.

Bax and Kip made their way down the sloping center aisle. The air smelled dead, as if school were out forever.

But things were starting to happen. Up on the lighted stage, men were opening folding chairs, with a lot of clacking and scraping noise. They were planting music stands among the chairs.

The secretary was putting slips of paper on the backs of the chairs, with cellophane tape.

Bax's legs felt unsteady. The people coming down the side aisles with instruments all looked old enough to be parents, even grandparents. Did he really belong here?

Kip was gazing up and around, as if he were trying to spot mysterious clues among the rows of turned-up audience seats or across the front of the balcony where spotlights were hanging. He had a new three-by-five notebook in one hand and a ball-point pen in the other.

Bax warned, "Somebody may think you're a suspicious character yourself, Kip, the way you're staring around."

"Takes one to know one. If anybody suspects me, they must have something to hide."

They kept their voices low. Sounds bounced and echoed around the massive walls.

Some of the violinists were opening their cases down in the front rows of the audience, leaving the empty cases there across the arms of the seats. Up on stage, a cellist who had a fiberglass case stood the case up behind the drum section and put his hat on it. It looked like a shapeless legless person standing there patiently.

Kip asked, "What are you going to do with your case while you're playing, Bax?"

"Keep it under my chair." His throat felt pinched as he wondered which chair was his.

"I'll sit in the rear of the audience. That will give me the broad overall view."

"Keep your eyes and ears open."

"Eyes, for sure," Kip promised. "But my ears aren't going to like this."

To get up to the orchestra seats, Bax had to climb a narrow stairway at the side of the stage. There were only a few steps, but it seemed like dozens.

He held his violin high so that he could thread across the first violin section to the section for the seconds.

Someone bumped into him and nearly knocked him over. "Hello, there." It was the woman who had made him go ahead of her at the auditions. "Nice to see they let you in."

"Thanks. You too," he mumbled. But was it all that nice for him? Was it perhaps only because he had a certain violin?

He checked the names taped to the chairs, working his way back, becoming more panicky with every strange name he saw. Wasn't his name even there, after all?

It was there. His place was the very last chair of the section. He stood there, feeling a long way out on the fringe of things.

The sounds of instruments, warming up and tuning, swirled around him in a mixture that made him tingle. Clarinets frittered up and down scales. French horns tooted, as though a-hunting they would go.

While Bax was unpacking his instrument, he recalled Kip's projected headline about him—**Youngest Member of Symphony**.

Bax stowed his case underneath his chair and straightened up. The man who was his partner at the stand slid into place. He was elderly and white haired, and he didn't even look at Bax. He took out his violin and played a melody to himself with his eyes closed. Bax watched him covertly. He must be **Oldest Member of Symphony**.

Bax stood up boldly and surveyed the whole orchestra. Mr. Fitting, the man who had auditioned so brilliantly before him, was concertmaster. That figured. Looking over the cellos, he found the woman who had bumped him today sitting on the last chair of the section, doing bowing exercises. Then he made the mistake of looking at the viola section.

There were five violas—and the last one was Susan Dodd. Susan was two days younger than he was. That blew the Youngest Member status. She was also a lot bigger than he was. She belonged with a viola, he reflected sourly. A viola is bigger than a violin, and plays down to five tones lower. And there are never as many willing viola players around as willing violinists—Susan probably got in without even having to audition.

He saw her raise her bow and start to wave at him, and he sat down quickly, ducking below the billowy hair of the large black woman who sat in front of him.

A voice spoke behind him. "Good day, young man. Glad to see you. And your violin."

Bax smelled a whiff of cigar, so he knew who it was even before he turned around. Mr. Hector Bolden stood between Bax's chair and the heavy blue curtains that hung along the side of the stage.

Was Kip watching? Frantically Bax's eyes searched the audience, but it was too dim out there to see much. He wanted to swing his arms in semaphore language to signal Kip a message. Hey! It's Mr. Bolden! A suspect! Observe! Take notes!

The elderly man, his stand partner, stopped fiddling and opened his eyes. "Eh, violin?"

The eyes were bleary, blinking. He looked surprised to find Bax next to him at all, and especially with, of all things, a violin. Then he nodded. "Ah. A Del Fiore."

Mr. Bolden leaned down, and the cigar odor threaded around Bax's nose like a wispy cloud. "What makes you say that?" Mr. Bolden demanded.

"The fleur-de-lis on the tailpiece, of course. Perhaps not a Del Fiore per se. But of the school of. My instrument, for example, is of the school of Jakob Stainer. You note the high arching of the belly, the breadth of the lower part. To be sure, Stainer did not found a school per se. He went quite mad, you know."

Bax knew. He had read about it. It was a heartbreaking story, how Jakob Stainer of Absam made marvelous violins but got so involved with suits for debt and suspicions of heresy and general tough luck, that he went out of his mind. Bax had seen a picture of a bench in front of the Stainer house that had holes in it for the ropes they had to use to tie the poor old raving man down.

Mr. Bolden asked Bax, "Did your aunt say it is a Del Fiore?"

Bax stammered, "She didn't say. She doesn't know."

Suddenly one of the trumpets blasted an arpeggio up to a piercing high C.

The snare drum crackled an earsplitting roll.

Enter the conductor, Mr. Emmet Hageman.

CHAPTER 10

Mr. Hageman leaped onto the podium. "Good afternoon, members of the Los Arboles Symphony Orchestra."

He was wearing a black turtleneck sweater. One lank lock of hair tumbled down his forehead toward his spectacles. Bax decided he was posing for the jacket of a record album—young conductor, casual but brilliant.

He went on, "We are going to work very hard, aren't we?"

Bax set up a scale of ten and gave him seven. Of course they were going to work hard. Any orchestra that didn't work hard wasn't worth playing in.

"But we're going to have fun. Aren't we?"

The smile was too phony. Bax lowered his rating to

five, then thought it over and upped him to seven and a half. After all, the conductor of a volunteer orchestra like this had to turn on the diplomacy and charm, had to promise fun. Every musician there could check right out if he thought it was going to be a bore.

Trumpeters were blowing *whuff*, tonelessly, warming their instruments. The tympanist was touching the kettledrum head with his finger, *tunk tunk*. Somebody flapped open a folder and spilled music to the floor with a slithery noise. People giggled.

Mr. Hageman quit being Mr. Personality and got down to brass tacks. "Oboe. Give the A."

There was dead silence. It was as if an alien force from space said, "Freeze," and nobody could move.

But somebody moved—somebody in the curtains, right behind Bax. He heard feet shuffling, someone stirring.

Was it Mr. Bolden? No, he could see Mr. Bolden in the audience, front row center.

Was it Kip on maneuvers? He couldn't see Kip anywhere out there in the dim auditorium.

The oboe spun an A into the stillness, a long nasal ribbon of pure tone.

Mr. Hageman said, "Tune."

Pandemonium broke loose. From rumble of bass to shriek of piccolo, there was so much blowing, scraping, and pounding, there could have been a brigade of robbers with rattling swords behind the curtains and Bax wouldn't have heard them.

Mr. Hageman whistled. Bax had to admire that. The piercing blast of that whistle was probably the only

51

sound in the world that could have cut through the tumult.

It brought silence again. "The overture."

Bax shouldered his violin, ready for the long drawn-out opening C of Beethoven's Overture to *Coriolanus*. Mr. Hageman gave the downbeat. The C swelled forth, grand, full. But then came the kicker, the sharp chord in F. And that was terrible! It was ragged, and sour. People gasped. Bax felt sick, as though someone had socked him in the throat.

Mr. Hageman looked sick too, then he pulled himself together, looked heavenward, and implored, "Forgive them, Ludwig."

This broke the tension. People laughed nervously and then relaxed. Bax raised Mr. Hageman's points up to eight and a half.

The rehearsal settled properly into drudgery, and Bax lost track of time till Mr. Hageman said, "Take fifteen."

Hastily, he packed up his violin and stowed it under the chair. He wanted to get out of sight before Susan Dodd could come galloping over and greet him like a relative. And he wanted to find Kip.

Where was Kip? Was he backstage? No. Was he out in the corridor? Bax pushed open the heavy stage door. The corridor was bright with sun streaming in from above the rows of gray lockers. There was no Kip.

He went into the audience part of the auditorium and scanned the gloom. There was no one.

Where was Kip? Growing anxious, Bax started trotting, past the water fountain. Dust danced in the sunlight. His footsteps echoed.

He rounded a corner, and saw someone ahead—just a quick shadow. "Hey, halt!" Bax broke into a run. "Tell me what you found out."

But the person ran too, lurching out of sight behind the athletic trophy case.

"Hey, wait!" called Bax.

He heard footsteps go slapping around a corner. He could hear clearly, they were very fast. It had to be Kip, being funny. Bax didn't think it was funny.

He followed, breath coming hard, smelling chalk and floor polish, passing the George Washington statue at a run.

The sound of footsteps ahead of him changed abruptly—from slap on tile to thud on concrete. The person was going down the stairs to the basement!

Bax started down, three steps, then stopped dead. He had no time to chase Kip around the Arroyo basement. Rehearsal would be starting. When Mr. Hageman said "Take fifteen," he did not mean time-out for track practice all over school.

Angry and hot, Bax raced back to the stage door. He could not bear to think of clattering into place late —calling attention to himself—having those sharp blue eyes of Mr. Hageman stab at him, maybe even having him make some caustic remark in front of the whole orchestra.

He yanked open the stage door and was relieved to hear the tuning-up sounds still villowing and booming.

Panting, trying to catch his breath, he stood backstage for a minute, leaning on a tall scenery flat that depicted a garden of pink roses with a sudsy-looking fountain bubbling in the middle of it.

"*Psst.*" Someone hissed from somewhere. The sound overrode the orchestra noises.

"*Psst.* You." There it was again. Where did it come from? It was like a ghost whispering above the painted garden.

Then it said "Bax!"

It was Kip! "Kip, where are you?"

"Up. Look up."

Bax looked up. Kip's pale face grinned down at him from a precarious perch on a catwalk overhead, alongside the ropes for hauling scenic backdrops up and down.

"Kip, what are you doing up there?" A thought rocked him—if Kip was up on that catwalk, Kip was not running around the basement. Then—who was?

Kip waved his notebook. "Getting the broad overall view. Bax, I saw him!"

"Who?"

"Your prowler. The man with all the hair."

Bax's heart jumped. "Did you recognize him? Do you know him?"

"I recognized him."

The racket of the orchestra was growing louder. Any second now, Mr. Hageman was going to whistle for starting. Bax would be late.

Impatiently he demanded, "Who is it? Hurry up. I've got to go. Who?"

Mr. Hageman whistled. There was silence onstage.

Kip said, "It's the devil."

CHAPTER

11

What did Kip think he was doing, anyhow—climbing ropes like a monkey, babbling about the devil, making Bax late? He tried to skulk into his chair and fish out his violin without being noticed.

But Mr. Hageman noticed. "You there, last chair second violin." He consulted his list of names. "Johann?"

"I'm called Sebastian." His voice was puny.

"See me after rehearsal, Sebastian."

"Yes, sir." Knots tied themselves in his stomach.

It was one thing to sit back and make judgment of a person, to set up a scale of ten and decide where he belonged, when there was no danger of being called to account. It was quite another thing to have that person haul you up for judgment on *you*. It made you feel quivery and limp.

What could Mr. Hageman do to him? He couldn't dock his wages; he wasn't getting any. He couldn't bust him back farther in the section; there wasn't any farther to go.

He could evict him! He built the scene vividly. He saw himself cringing in front of the podium. He heard Mr. Hageman passing the buck to Mr. Bolden by saying "The president of the Symphony Association has ordered: 'Out with all irresponsible kids.' "

With his mind in such a lather, he played wrong notes and inaccurate rhythms. Once he squeaked out a note where there was supposed to be silence. Mr. Hageman barked, "Sebastian! Count rests." He wanted to sink through the floor. Actually a lot of other people made mistakes too, but that was not any comfort.

The rehearsal ended in general gloom.

"We were hoping to schedule a public concert," said Mr. Hageman unhappily, "in five weeks. But there will have to be a great improvement over today's example. Take your music home. Practice."

The man at Bax's stand said, "I presume you will want the music, laddie?"

Bax shook his head grimly. "I don't presume I may even be here next week."

"Then I'll take it. Just to familiarize, of course. I don't need the practice per se." He eyed Bax oddly through half-closed eyes. "Take care of that violin, laddie."

People were muttering, clattering with their instruments, scraping chairs, drifting away. Bax packed up his violin and edged forward to the conductor's podium. And there stood Susan Dodd.

She said brightly, "He asked me to wait too."

"You?" Why should Susan have to wait?

Susan had a round face, bright hazel eyes, long blonde hair that lay shiny on her shoulders. She always hunched her chin downward as if she were trying to shrink. Bax always reached his chin upward, trying to stretch.

Bax glowered. He would have been the youngest if Susan hadn't moved in. And Susan wasn't dumb. She was always hot on Kip's heels for highest grades in the class.

Mr. Hageman was looking nervous. He kept staring toward Bax's violin as if he couldn't keep his eyes off it. "I just thought you ought to become better acquainted with one another."

Bax felt let down. All this buildup of fear and trembling—for a social introduction to a girl he'd known for years and never wanted to know in the first place.

Susan was saying brightly, "Oh, I've known Bax for ages. He's concertmaster of our school orchestra, where I play viola whenever the school viola is available."

She had the school viola in hand now, the case stenciled with *Prop'ty L A Jr Hi Orch*. Bax had been glad when the school orchestra director managed to loosen the Performing Arts budget up enough to buy that viola. Susan had been playing violin up to that time and was hot on Bax's heels for the position of concertmaster.

Mr. Hageman opened his mouth and shut it again,

looking disconcerted, as if he had thought he had a good idea, but it was going off the track. He leaned down to pick up his briefcase. Suddenly he snapped upright. "Who's there?"

Bax jumped. "Where?"

"In those curtains." He pointed to the heavy blue drapes that hung behind the chair where Bax had been sitting. "I distinctly saw those curtains move."

It must be Kip, casing the joint. Bax said hastily, "They're not moving now. Come on, Susan, we'd better go."

If he could hurry Susan out of there, then Mr. Hageman would exit too, and Kip could sneak out without being caught and questioned.

"But they did move," said Susan. "I saw it too. Somebody must be there."

Mr. Hageman jumped down from the podium. "I'll find out."

The curtains parted. Kip shuffled out and came over to join them. "It's me."

Mr. Hageman demanded, "Who are you?"

Bax said quickly, "It's a friend of mine, sir. Kip. Christopher Hatch, that is. Sir." He tried to remember to pour on the *sirs*. If you came on with *sir* heavy enough, adults didn't worry so much about potential delinquency.

"Christopher, what are you doing here?"

"Casing—" Kip started, but Bax kicked him in the ankle. "I mean—I am a music lover," he amended with an air of earnest virtue. "Sir."

Susan was staring at him. "You are? Since when?"

Bax knew that Susan knew that Kip always did crossword puzzles in Music Appreciation class.

"Since the formation of the cultural new Los Arboles Symphony," Kip told her, and then he added, "ma'am."

Susan blinked. "That's hard to believe."

Mr. Hageman nodded and smiled. "I am very glad to hear that. I hope you will come to all the rehearsals."

Kip gazed out toward the empty auditorium. "Not all rehearsals, I guess, sir. Sometimes I'll stay home and play records."

Susan snorted. "I've heard some of your records."

Bax tried frantically to get everybody into motion. "I think we have to go home now, we really have to leave. Good-bye, Mr. Hageman."

Mr. Hageman kept looking at Bax's violin case. "Take care of that violin, Sebastian."

"Yes, sir. I plan to."

The three of them left the stage and trudged silently up the long center aisle, across the wide echoing corridor, out into the summer heat. Bax was trying to figure out how they could shake off Susan. But Susan stopped.

Her eyes swung from Kip to Bax. "Now tell me, you two, what's this all about? There is something funny going on around here. Something very funny."

CHAPTER 12

They were standing on the high entrance porch of the school. Trapped between tall Susan and taller Kip, Bax felt like a low prickly pear cactus between two giant saguaros.

He stared around vacantly and tried to look innocent. "Something funny? I don't see anything funny."

There were a couple of fellows in gold helmets gunning a motorcycle around the parking lot, under the big school sign that said CONGRATS GRADS THE END BYE BYE.

"You know what I mean," said Susan. "Kip turns up pretending to be a big music lover. Mr. Hageman stares at your violin case as if he has X-ray vision and sees a machine gun in there. What's going on?"

Bax sighed. The oppressive odor of motorcycle exhaust hung in the air. He looked at Kip. Kip looked at him and shrugged. They were going to have to clue Susan in.

"It's the violin," said Bax. "My aunt loaned it to me because somebody tried to steal it from her."

"Somebody *what?*"

"Tried to steal it. She bought it in a weird little German shop, musty and dusty. She really didn't know what she was getting."

Susan offered breathlessly, "But then somebody slinky followed her home from the shop."

"Not quite." In spite of his annoyance, he warmed to his story. Susan was a terrific listener. "Anyhow, she got it home safely and peeled off the canvas cover and took a look at the case. This is some case."

"Can I see it?"

"Not now. I don't want to wrestle with undoing the snaps."

"What's Mr. Hageman got to do with it?"

"Mr. Hageman was traveling on the same boat with my aunt. He accompanied her on the piano when she played in the Ship's Concert. And then that night somebody came sneaking into her stateroom and tried to get the violin."

Susan shivered. "Mr. Hageman?"

"No, somebody with a lot of bushy hair."

"And she dumped the violin on you, Bax?" Susan's eyes were wide with admiration. "And you accepted? That's pretty brave."

Bax squared his shoulders. "What's more, somebody came prowling around when my aunt was playing, right here in Los Arboles, in my own trailer park. Somebody with a lot of wild hair. I almost caught him."

"That," said Kip sourly, "was prowler number one. You landed on prowler number two like a splashdown from space. I'm still sore."

Bax said, "I'm sorry."

"How noble of you. You are forgiven. Now for my report."

"Can you give it while we move along? We'll bake, just standing here."

Susan asked, "Can I walk with you guys as far as my turnoff?"

Bax didn't say anything, but Kip said generously, "Why not?"

The boys pushed their bicycles; Susan walked between them.

She said, "Report on what?"

"On my observations. My pose as the great classical music lover is actually a spy disguise."

"You didn't have me fooled."

Kip neatly flipped his little notebook open with one hand. "From my position on the catwalk, gazing downward, I noted the presence of the following: six bald heads, fourteen going bald, two Afros, seven blondes, nine brunettes, one pale blue, one sort of orange—"

"Any wild hair like the prowler?"

"I'm coming to that. At rehearsal break, I observed that the lady on last chair cello remained to practice—"

Bax said, "She needs it, she hasn't played for years."

"Likewise last chair viola—"

62

Susan said virtuously, "I'm always trying to improve."

"But last chair second violin disappeared. Johann Sebastian Barlow, where were you?"

"I thought you'd never ask." Bax prepared to spring his news. "I was looking for you."

"You found me."

"After you said '*Psst*' at me from above my head, when the break was all over. You'd better ask what I was doing *during* the break."

"Will the witness kindly tell the court, in your own words, just what you were doing during the break?"

Bax stayed silent a minute, to improve the dramatic effect. They passed a palm tree in which dozens of sparrows were holding a noisy conference.

"I was running all over the high school," he announced, "chasing a person I couldn't see."

Susan asked excitedly, "Somebody with a lot of hair?"

"The prowler prowls again," said Kip.

"I couldn't see hide *nor* hair. I thought it was you, Kip, being funny. Getting me to chase you, just to be nutty."

"I can be nutty without running," said Kip. "The kind of music you people were playing can drive me nutty just listening."

"I admit the rehearsal was pretty bad. But listen now, this is important. I was looking for you, Kip, and didn't find you. I just caught a glimpse of somebody, like a shadow, out in the corridor. I yelled—and he ran."

"Or she," said Susan. "Prowling isn't for men only."

"Anyhow, this person ran. Fast. Around corners, past old George." His voice rose as he relived the chase.

Kip kicked a rock off the sidewalk. "Would anyone in the court care to present a hypothesis as to who it was?"

Susan said, "I know who it wasn't."

"Who wasn't it?"

"Mr. Hageman. He was right on stage all the time, trying to straighten the French horns out on some transposition."

Bax was thinking. "You know who it could have been? A person I didn't see around after the first half of the rehearsal—"

"Present your hypothesis."

"Mr. Hector Bolden."

CHAPTER
13

Susan gasped. "Mr. Bolden? Can he run?"

"You're pretty fast, you know, Bax," said Kip. "I've seen you go the length of the soccer field almost as fast as I can with my long legs."

"Maybe Mr. Bolden was a soccer star in school."

They were nearing Susan's corner.

Kip said, "I bet I know who it was."

"Who?" Susan stopped on the street corner. "Tell me, tell me, I can't go home without knowing."

Kip gazed off toward Paiute Peak, where a pile of clouds hovered low. "I bet it was the devil."

"That's crazy," said Bax. "You can't see the devil; he's invisible."

"I've seen his picture. In your own encyclopedia about stringed instruments."

"Come on home and show me."

Susan said eagerly, "And then tell me about it at the next rehearsal." She swung away from them, along a street barren of trees or bushes, lined with boxlike apartment houses.

Bax grunted as they mounted their bikes. "Her we could do without. She is a pain."

"She has some good points," said Kip. "She listens creatively."

Bax didn't like being pulled two ways about people. He would rather either think they were absolutely great or not be able to stand them. It made life simpler.

"But have you listened to her? She's always being so dramatic. Like bragging about how she has her special library card out to the university."

"Don't you have one? Your mother works out there too."

"She's only there in the winter session. And she doesn't believe in special privileges for kids."

His mother taught some master classes in piano interpretation. Susan's mother, a widow, worked in the registrar's office all year round.

"You're about two millimeters taller than Susan," said Bax. "It gives you a different angle."

They pedaled to Bax's home, and his little room was like an oven. He switched on the air conditioner. The main cooler for the rest of the place didn't have much effect back there, so his father had installed a separate one for him in the ceiling vent. It lurched, went *bump*, then settled into a steady *sh-sh*, blowing cold.

"Here's the book, Kip." He pulled the encyclopedia from the shelf. The binding felt hot. "Find me the devil."

Kip sat on the floor. Bax flopped on the bed. Once you switched on the air conditioner, you were in a cocoon. There was no sound in the world but that soft insistent *sh-sh*.

"I found it!" Kip dumped the open book onto Bax's stomach.

Bax took one look at the figure on the page and knew who it was. It had hair in a mess, long black coat, skinny arms flailing with a violin and bow. "Kip, that's Niccolò Paganini."

"But it says something about the devil."

Bax read. "Sure, it does. It says he played so amazingly, some people thought he was diabolically inspired. Inspired by the devil, that means."

"I can figure that out."

"And it says this is an imaginative sketch as he might have appeared when rendering *Trillo del diavolo*, or *The Devil's Trill*, by Tartini."

"I saw him today," Kip insisted. "Lurking."

Bax scanned the text. "It couldn't have been old Niccolò himself. It says here he flourished from the late seventeen hundreds till his death in 1840. He couldn't flourish then and lurk now."

"Maybe it was a ghost." Kip put his feet up on the laundry hamper. "The ghost of Paganini looking for his long lost violin. The ghost of Beethoven looking for his papers."

"What papers?"

"Some old notes he made, and people made for

him. They got stolen after the war and smuggled out of East Germany. I read about it. Some were found, but some were missing, and then the missing ones were found."

"So why would a ghost be looking for something that isn't missing?"

"Well, our government was supposed to hand them over to the East German government where they belong. But I read that the handing-over ceremony has been postponed. That's the most recent news. I figure maybe that means they're missing again. This bulletin comes to you through the courtesy of the Christopher Hatch Read-everything-you-can-get-your-hands-on News Service."

Bax got up and shoved the encyclopedia back into place on the shelf. The binding had cooled down. Everything had cooled down, except his hot tangled brain. "That was no ghost today. Whoever I chased down the basement had real feet in real shoes."

Kip pulled his lanky length up from the floor. "I have to go. My uncle caught his limit of bass in Paiute Lake, and we're having a fish fry tonight."

"I think we're having meat loaf," said Bax gloomily. "Seems to me every time I sit down we're having meat loaf."

Kip grinned. "Wait till you commence the Growth Spurt. Everything will taste great. I could eat sawdust loaf."

One time when Bax's mother took him to the doctor, the doctor gave him a lecture on the Growth Spurt. You got it in adolescence. Some started it early. Some started it late.

Bax had a horrible fear that some, Bax Barlow by name, might never start at all.

"Kip, do you think I'll ever start growing?"

Kip laid a heavy hand on Bax's shoulder. "Why, certainly. Certainly indeed. Young man, I have every confidence in you. Just start doing push-ups and calisthenics every morning at five. Then run ten miles a day—uphill—"

"Oh, go fry a fish."

CHAPTER

14

At supper, his mother asked how rehearsal went.

Bax pushed meat loaf around his plate. "Terrible."

"Fine."

"Fine?" Hadn't she heard what he said? "But they want to try to put on a concert in five weeks. They can't unless we get an awful lot better."

"Early rehearsals are always bad," she said calmly.

"I thought it's dress rehearsals that are supposed to be bad."

"They are."

"Then when are rehearsals any good?"

"That's unpredictable." She gazed across the dining counter, up at the hood over the stove. "Things can quite suddenly jell, and you know it's all worth the effort."

Or maybe, thought Bax grimly, things can never jell, and it isn't worth the effort at all.

His father asked, "How did you get along with Daphne's violin? Were you compatible?"

Bax knew that cool humorous tone of voice. He knew how to answer it. "We got along great. We compatted like crazy."

Throughout that week, his practicing swung from high to low—high when the vibrato was rocking well and he was sounding like a pro, low when he was wishing he had the orchestra music to work on. But old Mr. Per Se had it. He felt uncomfortably pressured, having to go to rehearsal unprepared. And that kind of pressure was something new—because he didn't *have* to go to rehearsal at all, not like school orchestra rehearsals. He was in this by choice. It was his own idea. He had to get a whole new set of feelings.

On the morning of the day for the second rehearsal, while he was practicing, he glanced out the window and saw movement on the roadway. It was the familiar blue and white truck with a red stripe around the middle. Mail delivery.

He laid the violin on the bed and rushed outside. There was always mail for the Barlows. His father was a big subscriber. His mother was a big sender-for. And Bax took over everything for Occupant.

He opened the box and pulled out the day's haul. There was a magazine for his father, a brochure for *Occupant* announcing that You Can Retire Within Ten Years on an Adequate Income, and a letter for his mother—from Aunt Daphne!

He bounded into the house, shouting, "Hey, Mother," then stopped. She was at the piano, repeating an intricate trilling passage with her left hand, and making notes in a spiral notebook. He knew she was working on a demonstration of ornamentation for her piano seminar. He also knew she never wanted to be interrupted for anything less important than the house on fire.

But he had to know what was in the letter. "Mother, here's a letter for you."

"Basty, you know I don't—oh. From Daphne."

"Tell me if she says anything in it about Mr. Hageman."

She scanned. "Ah, here—'Emmet was so nice, so attentive, on the whole short flight. He acted just as he had at first on shipboard. Nervous as a cat, though.' "

"I'll bet," Bax murmured.

" 'He is coming up here to visit me—' Now isn't that sweet?"

Bax knew more than he was going to say about that. Mr. Hageman made the promise to visit while they were on the plane—while he had his eye on the brown canvas cover of the violin she was carrying—before he knew it was Bax's unimportant fiddle in there. But he knew different now. "Does she say anything about finding the bill of sale and sending it?"

"Good gracious, I had forgotten about that. I must write and remind her. Your father worries."

So do I, thought Bax, so do I.

He rustled up some lunch, but he wasn't hungry. He went on worrying. Part of him worried about Kip's devil, whoever that might be, sneaking around stealthily in the auditorium. And part of him worried about the music. At a first rehearsal, anybody ought to be forgiven for mistakes, because everybody is sight-reading. But by the second rehearsal, you were supposed to have done your homework. He hadn't.

Pedaling his bike along the hot street toward Arroyo High, he had a panicky moment when he wondered if his elderly stand partner might not come at all. In that case there wouldn't even be any music for him to play.

But the partner was there. His pale blue eyes opened wide, and his sparse white eyebrows arched up in surprise as Bax slid into place. "Why, hello, laddie. So you were not dismissed from our midst."

Bax yanked at the snaps of his case cover. He wanted to tell the man that he didn't really feel he was in anybody's *midst*, he felt more like barely allowed around the outskirts. "I'm still here."

The man was watching intently as Bax opened the case. "And how is your violin?"

Bax shot him a puzzled look. He sounded as if he were inquiring after the health of a frail patient who needed careful medical attention. "Fine, thanks." Then he added boldly, "How's yours? Feeling okay? No chills or fever, swollen strings, pain in the pegs?"

The man sniffed haughtily and put his violin up to his chin. "There is no call to be impertinent."

Bax wished he hadn't said it. It was stupid to antagonize the man he was stuck with at this stand. But there was no way of calling words back, once you had launched them.

There was no time to apologize even if he could

have thought of a reasonable way to do it. Mr. Hageman had leaped onto the conductor's podium and let out his piercing whistle. "Tune."

There was silence, and then came the long cool A from the oboe.

Suddenly Bax sensed something strange. It was what he had thought he heard before—a step and a stir—in the curtains behind him.

He knew it could not be Kip. Kip had said he couldn't stand two rehearsals in a row, and made Bax promise to come to his place and report anything worth reporting right after rehearsal.

Tensely he listened.

But whoever was there had gone.

CHAPTER 15

The first half of the rehearsal was a grind. Bax had trouble but so did the French horns. He missed some entrances, but it didn't show, as he was one of so many violins. The first bassoon missed some entrances, and that did show.

By rehearsal break, the general orchestra mood was grimmer than ever.

Bax loosened the horsehairs of his bow, as he had been taught always to do, and snapped the bow into its place in the case lid.

Glancing across the orchestra he could see the blonde head of Susan as she stood up at the back of the viola section. Was she coming over here? How could he dodge her?

The curtains! He could lurk in the curtains and see

75

how Kip's devil, whoever he was, felt in there, invisible. He might even still be there.

He snapped the snaps, slid the case under his chair, jumped up, and ducked into the voluminous velvet.

No one else was there. But it was a great hiding place, all right. It was totally dark within those heavy folds, and he could hardly hear a sound. The smell was dusty, with a faint sweetness like stale perfumed stage makeup. The curtains dragged all the way to the floor. If anyone lurked in there, even his shoes could not be seen.

Suddenly a sharp poke rammed his ribs. He coughed, making a muffled choking sound.

Ouch—it came again. Then he felt the curtains being pawed at, being yanked every which way, rubbing against his face, pulling across his back.

He grabbed at the thick folds, trying to stay hidden. But it was no use. The curtains parted and there stood Susan.

"Well, well, do tell," she said noisily. "It's the devil himself. Where's your pitchfork, Bax?"

"Don't be so loud," he growled angrily. "I was lurking in there for a purpose."

Susan planted her hands on her hips. She had on a long prairie-type dress, with big puff sleeves. She looked enormous. "For the purpose of getting away from me, I suppose."

Bax's stand partner had been playing a slow melody, with his eyes closed. Now he opened his eyes and turned around. "My goodness gracious. Aren't you two young persons friends?"

76

Bax pushed at his hair, trying to smooth it down. None of this was any of the strange old man's business. "Oh sure, we're friends."

"No, we're not," said Susan. "I want to be, but Bax here is only friends when Kip is around to take the curse off."

The man hung his violin by the scroll on the ledge of the music stand, and turned to face them. He cleared his throat. "Allow me to inform you of the opinions I have formed on this subject. According to my observations, friendship per se is not of the essence."

Bax was in no mood for lectures on anything per se. "I think what I need is a drink of water. Come on, Susan, let's hit the water fountain."

The man made no effort to hold them for his observations. "Yes, indeed, you go on out, an excellent idea. Take a long stroll through the building." He was smiling very oddly.

As he opened the heavy stage door, Bax looked back. The man was watching them.

Out in the corridor, the sun slanted down from the windows above the lockers, blindingly bright.

Susan stood still, folding her arms. "You don't want a drink of that water. It'll be lukewarm and taste terrible. You just didn't want to be seen in there hanging around with me."

"I'm thirsty," Bax said stubbornly. The inside of his mouth did feel dry, so he wasn't really lying.

"Okay, over there's the fountain." She marched along beside him like a big inescapable bodyguard. "Now tell me. What about Kip's devil?"

"Nothing. There's no devil."

"There's somebody. You chased somebody. Kip saw somebody. Somebody that reminded him of the devil."

Bax turned on the water of the fountain, a feeble stream. "It was somebody that reminded him of a picture in my encyclopedia. A picture of Niccolò Paganini."

"Paganini? But he's dead."

"He's been dead a long time." Bax bent over the fountain to drink. The water was lukewarm, as she had predicted, and tasted terrible.

"I'm thirsty too." Susan bent to drink, then straightened up and shrieked. "That's awful. Yuck. That's the worst-tasting stuff I ever tasted in my whole life."

Bax looked up and down the corridor, feeling embarrassed. He was relieved to see that there was no one in sight. "Cut the dramatics, Susan, it's not all that bad."

"Yes, it is. Anyway, that's the way I react. I can't help it if I'm an emotional type."

Why did she have to make herself out to be so special, so important? "Everybody's emotional. Only they don't have to put on such a big act about it."

"You put on a big act while you were telling about your chase through the school, running after the ghost or whatever."

He flushed. "That was a big chase."

"Show me where you went. Come on, instant replay." Her eyes brightened. "Here's the water fountain. From here he went—thataway?"

"Thisaway." Bax trotted toward the athletic trophy case. The thrill of last week's pursuit began building up in him all over again. "And on, this way, toward the George Washington statue—"

"Weren't you afraid? On TV he would have had a gun."

There she went, being dramatic again. "On TV I would have had a gun too. Here he turned—"

"Or she."

"And this is where I lost him." He stopped at the head of the stairway to the basement.

Susan leaned over the railing, gazing, listening. There was no sound but a fly buzzing at a high window and their own breathing.

"He's down there still," she whispered. "Stumbling in the darkness, a lost soul wailing for a way out. And then he's going to turn into ectoplasm, and he'll come oozing up the stairs, a strange gray form—"

Bax shuddered. Everything was already very wierd and spooky, and she was making it worse.

He shook himself. "Hey, we've got to go." He turned and started to run. "If you've made us late—"

She panted alongside him. "*I* made us late? *You* went right along, Johann Sebastian. It's as much your fault as mine."

They pelted through the empty halls. Bax felt as if he were traveling in convoy with an elephant. At last he pulled open the stage door, telling her, "The whole thing was your idea."

"Oh sure, I'm the one that's all the way wrong. I'm the pain in the neck—"

The orchestra was tuning. Bax was glad the noise was so loud he didn't have to answer. She sounded near tears. If she was going to cry, the orchestra noise would drown that out too.

He determined angrily to get away fast after rehearsal and not get stuck with going along with her on the way home.

Feeling hot and irritated, he planted himself on his chair. His partner was industriously practicing a fast passage and did not even look up.

Bax pulled his violin case up across his knees.

The denim cover flapped loose. It was not snapped shut!

A feathery chill rippled up his spine. Hadn't he closed it properly? But he would have sworn he had. He remembered hurrying, to get it all closed up before Susan could come galloping over. With trembling fingers, he opened the case—and got a real shock.

The bow hairs were tightened! The bow was ready for playing.

But he knew he had loosened them. He always did. He would never put away a bow that was tightened up.

CHAPTER 16

Bax could hardly wait for rehearsal to be over, to get away and talk to Kip.

It seemed hours before Mr. Hageman finally flapped shut the last musical score on his stand. "Next week," he said grimly, "will be decision time. Whether we can put on a concert—or whether we can't."

Bax's stand partner turned toward him. "You certainly need to take the music home and practice, do you not, laddie?"

So his agitation had been pretty obvious. "Yes, sir, I need the music." And a few explanations!

Not even glancing toward Susan, he packed up fast and headed for Kip's place.

As he turned into Kip's driveway, a car came barreling along behind him and shrieked to a screeching halt across the street. Startled, Bax turned. Then he grinned. It was the red car that had followed him after the auditions. Angela May had obviously had her brakes fixed now, and wanted the whole neighborhood to know it.

Kip was out watering the lawn. He was sitting on a cushion on a white iron bench, spraying around with the hose.

Bax parked his bike by the laundry yard.

Kip turned the hose on Bax as he approached, soaking him from head to foot. It felt lovely. He sat on the hot cushion beside Kip and stretched out, evaporating. "You should have come to rehearsal, Kip."

The transistor radio under the bench was belting out a thumping beat. "I told you, I can't take Ludwig van Bake-oven every week."

"You should have been there to observe at the break. Listen, Kip: Somebody tampered with the violin while I wasn't there."

"Tampered with—" Kip jerked the hose straight up overhead, then whipped it down, saying, "I better not do that, I'll drip on my radio. Bax, why weren't you observing? Where were you? Or Susan? Wasn't she in her place trying to improve?"

"She was running around the school with me." A wave of embarrassment washed over him as he remembered. "She wanted to see where I had gone when I took off after the invisible runner last week."

Kip groaned. "Off on the great chase trace. Meanwhile, back at the auditorium—"

"Somebody meddled with the violin. I could tell.

They tightened the bow. They didn't close the snaps of the cover."

"And you weren't there to watch," scolded Kip. "It could have been Mr. Hageman, Mr. Bolden, Mr. Devil—"

"It could have been anybody. But why? What do they want? Kip, you've got to come with me to the next rehearsal and keep a close watch."

"You realize you're asking a lot."

"Come on, at least through the break."

"Well, all right. But only till after the break. Then you're on your own."

The sun beat down on them. A roar billowed high overhead as a couple of jets from the nearby air base trailed each other through the sky.

"Hey, Kip, my mother had a letter from my aunt. She says Mr. Hageman was all friendly and lovey-dovey on the plane trip."

"I'll bet he was. He thought she had the violin."

"And she says he said he's going to visit her."

"I'll bet he isn't. Because now he knows *you* have the violin."

"I'll bet you're right."

"And I'll bet your daffy aunt's next letter is going to be written to you."

"Why me?"

"Because Mr. Hageman won't come. And she won't know why. And you're the only person in the world she can ask about it."

Bax frowned. "But what can I tell her? I don't know what's going on either."

"It'll take some thinking," said Kip. "That's why I

like to sit and water the lawn, it's so great for thinking. I don't really have to water it by hand, I could turn on the automatic sprinkler and spray the whole yard at once. In fact, I think I will." He dropped the hose and groped under the bench for his radio.

Kip waited till Bax was wheeling away, then picked up the hose and directed a hard cold stream directly on his back.

"Thanks," yelled Bax. "I needed that."

He pedaled on home with his head full of problems. He didn't like writing letters anyhow. What could he tell Aunt Daphne if she asked? Nothing that made any sense.

Kip came along to the next rehearsal.

By squinting at the dusky cavern of the auditorium from where he sat on stage, Bax could just make out Kip slumped in the back row, only a pale head out there. He could see Mr. Bolden glowering in the front row, frowning and fidgeting as if he were worried.

As Bax let his eyes rove, he suddenly spotted something new—a person in the balcony! He was sure there had never been anyone up there before. He squinted and stared, trying to figure out what kind of face it was. But it looked like only half a face.

At the break, he packed his instrument hurriedly, slipped it under his chair, and scooted back to Kip. "Kip, there's a new person at this rehearsal, up in the balcony. There never has been a person in the balcony before."

"Let's get up there and have a look at him. Or her."

"It has only half a face," Bax whispered as they sidled bumpily past the folded seats and out into the aisle.

"Which half?"

"I couldn't tell. It's hard to see from the stage."

Tiptoeing carefully, they mounted the dark stairs that led to the balcony. Bax led the way, keeping one hand on the cold rough wall.

"Hurry up," Kip breathed into his ear from behind.

"I'm trying—" But he tried too hard. He miscalculated the last step and stumbled with a noisy thud into the side aisle.

The balcony stretched empty before them, a huge sloping checkerboard. The seats were all folded up except one, in the middle, halfway up.

"Clumsy me," Bax mourned. "I scared him out."

"Maybe not. Maybe he was already gone. He'd be smart to get out and escape any more of your so-called music."

Bax sighed. "I guess the orchestra still doesn't sound too good."

They made their way down the steep steps to the front of the balcony and looked out over the auditorium.

"Nobody is doing anything funny." Kip waved his notebook down toward the audience. "See, there's Mr. Hageman arguing with Mr. Bolden in the front row, both present and accounted for."

"And there's my stand partner playing lullabies to himself."

"And I don't see even the tiniest ripple in the curtains behind your chair." Kip pocketed the notebook.

"Nothing can happen from here on, while you have the violin under your chin. So I'll do like your mysterious Half-face, I'll take off. I see Mr. Bolden has the same idea—there he goes. Well, be seeing you."

"Be seeing you."

Bax stood a minute alone, gazing at the pattern of chairs, stands, instruments, on the stage. The kettle-drum heads looked like enormous flat saucers. Bass viols lay on their sides at the rear like sleeping animals. His own violin case under the chair at the very end of the second violin section looked small and insignificant.

Would he ever feel as if he really belonged there? Would he always feel like a kind of afterthought, only allowed in on tolerance?

Head down, hands in pockets, he trudged down the long dark way to the stage again. But as he made his way to the chair, his head jerked up, seeing someone backstage in the gloom. It was Half-face!

He could see now that the half was the upper half, because the lower half was obscured by a bushy beard. He was a tall fellow, wearing dark clothes that were hard to identify, but with occasional glints around the knees as if there were something shiny sewed on. He was sitting on a crate, just lounging there.

Bax got his violin out and tuned the strings, wondering about this new observer.

Then he forgot about observer or mystery or anything else, because the miracle happened. It happened suddenly, unpredictably, gloriously. The magic for which they had all been striving so hard came to life! The tone sang strong, the chords crackled brilliantly—

the Los Arboles Symphony Orchestra sounded absolutely magnificent.

Bax felt eight feet tall. And he felt for the first time as if he truly belonged and was a real part of it.

Mr. Hageman slapped his music shut with a smack of triumph.

There was a brief spatter of hands clapping backstage. Bax swiveled to look. Half-face, back there in the darkness, had applauded—and then he immediately dived for the door and ran out!

Mr. Hageman wasn't paying any attention to that. "How about it, people? Shall we schedule a concert? All in favor signify."

Trumpets fanfared. Drums thudded. Feet stamped. All in favor signified very noisily.

Bax felt like soaring on wings, high among the ropes overhead.

But Mr. Hageman brought him down to earth. "Sebastian."

The glorious feeling wrenched away abruptly. "Sir?"

"See me before you go."

Bax packed his instrument and slunk over to the podium slowly, feeling like a culprit on trial for some crime he couldn't remember committing. Now what had he done?

As it turned out, he had not done anything. Mr. Hageman wanted him to do something. "We will have to print programs. We will need program notes. Sebastian, I am assigning you the project of looking up material on Beethoven, and especially on *Coriolanus*."

Bax looked at the floor. This sounded like school-work.

"Our overture is not for the Shakespeare play, of course," Mr. Hageman went on, "but you might look into the Shakespeare anyhow. Also other Beethoven overtures. *Egmont*, for instance. Do some library research." He was beaming as if an order to do library research ranked on a level with a ticket to Game of the Year.

"Actually," Bax mumbled, "I'm not all that crazy about libraries."

"Get your friend the music lover to help you. Christopher. Didn't I see him here earlier?"

"You saw him." Bax refrained from adding, "But you didn't hear what he said about the way your orchestra sounded in the first half of the rehearsal."

If only Kip could have heard how they sounded in the second half! Mr. Bolden had left and missed it too. Only the mysterious Half-face had been so impressed he applauded—then hurried out.

Mr. Hageman was packing music into his briefcase. "I understand that this town has a city library and a county library. Might there be some way you also could have access to the university library?"

"There might." Susan had her special library card. But she had already left, mad at him. He ought to feel pleased that she felt insulted and left him alone. But he didn't. He felt squirmy. Oddly, he felt as if he would almost have rather had her hanging around and pushing herself into the act.

"Splendid." Mr. Hageman leaned over toward Bax

as if he were having a great idea. "They will have musical scores at the university. You can take that—your—violin out there with you, and try playing some of the music."

Something in Bax's mind went click. Mr. Hageman seemed entirely too pleased with this idea. Did he *want* Bax and the violin to travel, to move out of the accustomed orbit of home and rehearsal, home and rehearsal?

"I'll try the city library first," he decided. "If I hurry, I can get there before closing today."

He tucked the folder of music under his arm and clumped down the narrow steps at the side of the stage.

A vague plan was stirring in the back of his mind, an idea, still fuzzy and formless, for forcing a showdown with the mysterious person who was after the violin. But the plan would involve getting out to the university. And getting out to the university would involve Susan. And Susan was mad at him.

CHAPTER 17

At the city library, Bax sat on a low chair at a high table, digging into Shakespeare.

Coriolanus, he found, was a Roman general who seemed to spend most of his time on stage yelling at people. "Boils and plagues plaster you o'er," he shouted at the men under his command. "You souls of geese—"

He was just deciding it was no wonder they let the guy rush into the hostile city of Corioli all by himself, when he became aware of loud whispering in the stillness of the library.

The librarian on duty at the desk was a high school boy Bax knew. He was saying, "There is no charge for a library card, sir, but you will have to have proof of residence. A utility bill, for instance."

Bax looked up. The man in front of the librarian was tall and thin. He said nervously, "But I am new in town."

It was Mr. Hageman!

Bax had had all the Shakespeare he wanted by then, so he closed the book, picked up his violin case, and went over to the desk. "I know this person. He conducts the new symphony orchestra."

"Oh, hi there, Barlow. Well, with that identification, I'm sure we can issue—"

"I don't have time now," said Mr. Hageman hastily. "I just—remembered something."

He hurried out. The librarian stared after him. "What's with him? He wants a card, he doesn't want a card."

Being addressed by his last name had given Bax a neat lift. "Good question. What's with him?" If Mr. Hageman really wanted a library card, he could have got one and stuck around and done his own program note research.

"And what's with you, Barlow? What were you doing over there in English Lit. on vacation time?"

"Looking up something for the symphony. What I really need is stuff on Beethoven."

"Sorry, we're pretty weak on Music here. We run heavy to Mystery and Western. Try the county."

After rehearsal the following week, Bax tried the county.

The county library, he found, ran to Art—expensive Art. Most of the resort hotels that brought the money into Los Arboles were situated outside city limits but in the county, so the tax income was lavish. It looked as though any volume of art reproductions that weighed over three pounds and cost over thirty dollars landed on the county library shelves.

He finally found Music, around behind Theater. There were a number of volumes on Beethoven. In fact, there seemed to be too many volumes on Beethoven.

He leafed through one and spotted *Egmont*, which Mr. Hageman had mentioned. Egmont was a real person, a hero of Flemish resistance against Spain a few centuries ago. Egmont might even be interesting. But Bax was stuck with Coriolanus, "of doubtful legend."

He wished he knew how much Mr. Hageman expected him to dig out. One volume appeared to be so thick and full that it must have everything about Beethoven that anybody could want to know, and then some. He pulled it from the shelf and looked for a place to settle down and study.

There was a red beanbag chair in a corner nearby, under a spreading collage made of pink and orange plaster and rocks and feathers and torn newspaper. He settled down in the beanbag chair with the heavy book, and started to seek for facts.

Born 1770, died 1827. Father made him practice piano for hours and tried to push him as a child prodigy. Later he became famous as a piano player, then as a composer. He rebelled against all tyranny, championed freedom for humanity.

Was that the sort of stuff a person should copy for program notes? Or was everybody supposed to know that much already?

He flipped through toward the back of the book—and sat up, electrified. Here was what Kip had been talking about—the famous Conversation Notebooks!

Beethoven had gone deaf, and in order to carry on conversations, he used the kind of method that Bax's neighbor, Mr. Richter, used, except that Mr. Richter had a slate, and you wrote in chalk that was erased. Beethoven used notebooks and ink, and hung onto every scrap.

About two hundred sixty of them finally landed in the *Staatsbibliothek,* the state library—now in the Eastern Zone of Germany. After World War II, they were stolen and smuggled over to the West—then discovered and returned to the East. "To the best of current knowledge," he read at the conclusion, "all have been restored."

"No," Bax muttered. Things had happened since that book was published. He remembered Kip telling about it—how some more of the Notebooks had turned up recently and were supposed to be restored to the Eastern Zone—but the restoration ceremony had been "postponed."

Staring thoughtfully into space, he suddenly saw a person over in the Music section. Quickly Bax lifted the book to hide his face and peered warily out around the edge of it.

The person he saw was Half-face, the man who had been at rehearsal in the balcony and had applauded briefly when the music sounded so good. He had on a fringed jacket with beaded decorations. He wore silver and turquoise bracelets, and turquoise rings. Bax could see now what had glinted around his knees—he wore blue jeans with a flower pattern in rhinestones embroidered over the lower part. On his feet were thong sandals. As Bax watched, the man flipped a book shut, replaced it on the shelf, and turned to leave.

Who was he? Why had he been creeping around the rehearsal? Bax kept the big book up in front of his face as the man passed by. Then he slipped from the beanbag chair, silently put the Beethoven book down, and followed the man at a careful distance.

Thick carpeting kept footsteps quiet, but the stairs were uncarpeted. Bax hid behind a column at the top of the stairway, listening to the *slap-slap* of the sandals going down the stairs.

It was peculiar how the man's motions did not go with his clothes. He walked stiffly, with small precise steps. A person in a swinging outfit like that would be expected to lounge loosely, to slop down the stairs with his elbows flapping.

Bax slopped on down with his own elbows flapping and out the door into a solid wall of heat. It was like being dumped into a world-size skillet to fry.

Sun blazed in a sky without a cloud. He saw the man turning the corner of the street ahead.

He fumbled with his bike lock. It was almost too hot to handle. He had a towel for the seat, and two washcloths for holding the hand grips.

He rolled along the street toward the corner. If the man looked around, Bax hoped he would not see anything too suspicious about a kid on a bike, just wobbling along and going pretty slow. He should realize that wobbling slow was all anybody could be expected to do in a hundred and sixteen degrees of heat.

But the man was out of sight. Where was he? Had he lost him?

He pedaled forward like a racer past a vacant area, then braked to a stop, skidding in a cloud of sand. Had he seen someone cutting through that vacant area?

He doubled back around the next corner. Yes, there he was, walking along stiffly, holding his arms at his sides and looking straight ahead.

The man made his way to one of the older residential sections. Small homes were set back in yards baked brown. Occasionally Bax would lean against a dying cottonwood tree and wait, so as not to pull up on his quarry too closely. But the shadows of the trees were just as hot as the beating sun.

There was something suspicious in the fact that the the man was walking at all. Practically nobody in Los Arboles walked, especially in summer. People had cars, and as many as could afford it had their cars air-conditioned. Bax would expect anybody in that kind of clothes to have a motorcycle at least.

But the man walked on—till he finally turned in at a dilapidated-looking pink house on a corner.

Bax waited awhile, staying out of sight around the corner, feeling roasted. Then he cruised past the house, hoping he looked idle and uninterested. There were four signs around the house. One was out on the front lawn, leaning crooked, a wooden sign saying FOR SALE. The paint was cracked, as if the sign had been there a long time.

The next sign was cardboard, tacked up on the porch pillar, saying Rooms To Rent, and under that another one, No Vacancy.

The biggest sign was painted on the glass of the front window, covering the whole window. It read Big Daddy's Practice Pad— and Big Daddy and a lot of little daddies must have been practicing in there at that minute. Bax could hear steady pounding and blasting and wailing of rock music, so loud it carried out through closed doors and windows. It was Kip's kind of music, not Bax's.

Why would anybody who stayed with Big Daddy hang around a symphony rehearsal?

CHAPTER 18

After some days of pondering, Bax went to see Kip. He was directed upstairs. Kip was packing.

"Bax, I've been trying to get you on the phone. Where have you been?"

"In libraries." He sat on one of the twin beds in Kip's spacious room. "Mr. Hageman wants me to find stuff for program notes for the concert."

Kip stopped still, holding a pile of T-shirts. "You're going to give a concert? You want people to pay to listen to you?"

"Kip, you should have heard us after you left. We were terrific, all of a sudden."

"Sure, you were." Kip dropped the T-shirts into his suitcase. "And it's twenty degrees outside, and we all need fur coats."

"We *were* terrific, whatever you think. Only I'll admit we don't sound like Big Daddy."

"Who's Big Daddy?"

"A bunch of noise. The man with half a face lives there."

"You never told me which half."

"Upper. Beard."

"That figures. Look, what I've been trying to phone you about is to say good-bye for a while. We're going up to my uncle's place on Paiute Lake."

"You're leaving me all alone with all the weird stuff that's going on? Just when I'm getting an idea for a plot, a kind of trap." He had counted on Kip to help him work out details.

"You'll have to spring the trap yourself. You can tell me all about it at the fish fry."

"What fish fry?"

"The one I'm inviting you to. Come to supper when I get back. That will be a week from tomorrow."

"The night before the concert." How many things were going to happen between now and then? "Okay, I'll come."

"I want to invite Susan too."

Bax brightened. "Can I ask her for you? I'll see her at rehearsal tomorrow." This gave him a great chance to get on the good side of Susan again.

"You can ask her. But you won't see her tomorrow."

"Why won't I?"

The sound of a voice sailed up from downstairs: "Christopher!"

98

Kip yelled, "I'm almost ready." Then he went on, "Susan won't be at rehearsal."

"Susan's always at rehearsal."

"Not the next one." Kip trotted to his neatly organized desk and picked up the morning newspaper, folded to a page of local miscellany. "Read all about it."

String Clinic at Music Camp, said the headline.

Wagon Pass Music Camp was holding a week-long clinic for teachers of stringed instruments in the public schools. The director of the Los Arboles Junior High School orchestra was going to present demonstrations—with particular emphasis on the viola.

Bax pounded his fist on the paper. "So there goes the school viola, up to music camp. Susan won't have an instrument. Susan won't be at rehearsal."

The voice from below soared upward again. "Chris! Kip! Move!"

"I'll move along too," Bax said.

Kip was leaving. Susan wasn't coming to rehearsal. He was all alone, deserted.

The next morning, he got a letter that informed him that one person, at any rate, was not deserting—Aunt Daphne. True to Kip's prediction, she wrote to Bax. "What's going on with that conductor of your orchestra?" she demanded—as if he could possibly tell her. "He's on, he's off. He's friend, he's foe. He said he was coming to visit me, now he writes that he is so tied up with concert preparations, he is not coming. Well, I'm coming—to that concert. I've got to find out what he is really capable of. Sometimes quite great musicians are slightly psycho—after all, look at me. Brace your

99

parents for my arrival." The date and time of her arrival were going to be exactly during the final rehearsal, the day before the concert.

She didn't say a word about the bill of sale. Bax wondered if he ought to take the violin out to Mr. Rucci for an appraisal. He had never seen Mr. Rucci. He only knew about his violin shop. He had made an appraisal on a violin that a girl at school got as a gift. But Mr. Rucci lived a long way out Rancho Road. It would be such a long hot uphill ride.

He toiled through the first half of the next rehearsal with the feeling that it was going on forever. By the time Mr. Hageman announced the break, he felt as if they had been playing for eight hours and had eight more to go.

He was packing up his violin when he felt that a large billowing person was brushing past him. He looked up. "Susan!"

"I'm not speaking to you," said Susan.

"I want to talk to you."

"That's a switch I do not believe." She swept on toward the stage door.

He fumbled hurriedly, closing the case. "Wait for me."

But she wasn't waiting. He jammed the case under his arm and followed her out.

She was heading for the water fountain. Bax put on his best soccer field sprint to get there first and turn the water on for her.

She bent to drink, then sputtered. "That's worse than it was three weeks ago! Ack. That's awful, absolutely awful." Her loud voice bounced and echoed through the warm stuffy air.

"Don't—" He was starting to tell her not to make so much noise but decided this was the wrong time for that. "Don't drink it, then."

"But I already did, dum-dum. What are you carrying your violin with you for?"

"To protect it. Somebody meddled with it that time you and I were out running around here."

"Meddled with it! A development! And you didn't tell me."

"Well, you see, I—"

"Don't apologize. You don't want to tell me things. You don't want to be seen with me."

"Susan, look—"

" 'Look,' he says. As if I could help looking. I'm always looking over the tops of practically everybody, I'm so tall. You just don't like hanging around with me because I'm a giantess and you're a shortie."

Anger flared. "I can't help being short, can I?"

"Not yet. But you will. You'll start the Growth Spurt. You'll shoot up. But me, I won't change. Do you think I like being a giantess? Do you think it makes me feel superior and above other people? Is that what you think?"

"I don't think anything." But he was thinking. He was thinking that he never had thought about it from Susan's point of view. He had just assumed that the only point of view that ought to matter to anybody in the world was his own.

"Tell you what," he offered desperately. "When

I'm six feet five, I'll be nice to you. I'll bow at your feet and offer you my sword and service."

"You're laughing at me."

"I am not. Why would I laugh at anybody twice my size?"

She considered that. "I suppose you wouldn't, if you had good sense. So you're going to be my loyal subject when you're six feet five?"

"That's a promise."

"Well, I won't be holding my breath." She still wasn't friendly, but at least she was speaking to him. "You said you wanted to talk to me."

"To ask you how come you're here."

"Here? At rehearsal? I *play* in this orchestra, remember?"

"But you play viola. Didn't the director take the school viola up to music camp?"

She smiled. Now she did look as if she thought herself superior. "Do you think that's going to stop me?"

"It would have stopped me," said Bax. "What are you playing on?"

"My violin."

"But how can you? Viola plays five tones lower than any violin can reach."

"I tuned all the strings down five tones. G down to C, and so on, up to E down to A. Clever, yes?"

"Clever. Yes." He never would have thought of that. "But how does it sound?"

She sighed. "Soggy."

"I'm not surprised."

"But that violin sounds soggy anyhow."

"You mean—it's not good?" Light bulbs were

102

going on in his brain. Susan had her violin—Susan's violin was not much good—all this was building right into the scheme that had been stirring around in his mind.

"It's rotten. I was supposed to get a new one, but then—well, it was just before my father died. And we couldn't afford it. So I took over the school viola."

"Is yours insured? Is it? Tell me."

"Of course it's insured. What are you getting so steamed up about? It's far overinsured. My dad never did anything by halves. In fact, when you brought your violin—"

"My aunt's."

"—your aunt's violin out here so carefully, I thought wouldn't it be nice if somebody would steal mine while I'm out here. I could use the insurance money to buy a viola of my own."

Bax lowered his voice to a mysterious tone. "Maybe something can be arranged."

"What have you got up your sleeve?"

"A plan. Can you get me into the university music library this afternoon?"

"So that's it. I knew you must want something."

"I want another thing, too. I want to invite you to a fish fry."

"I don't believe you."

"Actually it's Kip's invitation. He's gone up to his uncle's place on the lake, and he wants you and me to come to supper when he gets back. A week from tonight."

"Now, that I can believe. Good. Kip will tell me what's going on. He talks to me. Not like you."

Bax choked back a desire to point out that he had

103

been talking to her this whole rehearsal break. "But you and I will be the ones with the news to tell, Susan. I'm hatching a plot."

"A plot with me in it?"

"I couldn't do it without you. It's pure luck that you've got your violin today."

"But why? What's the idea?"

"Hey, it's time for us to go in."

"But now I'm dying to know what you're up to."

"You'll find out. So will some other people."

CHAPTER 19

Back in place in the orchestra for the second half of the rehearsal, Bax had to give himself a pep talk, to rev up his courage for what he was about to do. Up to now, back here in the last row, the main thing he did not want to do was to call attention to himself. But now he wanted to make everybody pay attention. Anybody who was present—or lurking—who wanted to know the whereabouts of the violin was being given notice.

Mr. Hageman whistled for quiet and ordered the oboe's A.

Bax raised up his hand and waved his bow. But that didn't work. Mr. Hageman just said, "Tune."

He waited out the tuning racket till Mr. Hageman whistled again. In the silence, Bax stood up. "Mr. Hageman?"

Mr. Hageman glowered. "Sebastian. What's wrong?"

"Nothing's wrong, sir." He wished his voice wouldn't threaten to squeak. "I just want to ask, can I speak to you after rehearsal?"

"Yes, yes, of course you can." Mr. Hageman opened his music impatiently.

Bax pushed on, even though his voice did squeak. "It's about me, and Susan from the viola section, taking our instruments out to the university. We want to try some music—the way you suggested—"

Mr. Hageman looked at him sharply. "You're taking the—your—violin out to the university today? How? Is someone driving you?"

"We're going on the bus."

He saw Mr. Bolden, who had been strolling up the center aisle of the auditorium, stop and turn around to face the stage. Then he turned around again and hurried away.

Mr. Hageman gave Bax a stern look. "All right, all right. If you plan to go, just go. We can't waste rehearsal time talking about it. Rehearsal time is valuable—we have preparation for the concert—"

Feeling shaky, Bax sat down, while Mr. Hageman went on to waste several minutes of valuable rehearsal time telling them why rehearsal time should not be wasted..

There, he had done it. Now if anybody wanted to track the violin, they knew where to follow. Mr. Hageman heard him and Mr. Bolden and his stand partner and any devil who might be in the curtains and Halfface, if he was around in the shadow.

Susan raced over to him after rehearsal. "Bax, what got into you? What made you stand up and advertise our trip like that?"

Here she went again, asking questions where he didn't want to answer them. "I'll explain," he growled.

"Oh sure, outside again. Don't sit and talk to me in here, somebody might think we're friendly."

His stand partner was holding his violin on his knee and watching them as if they were putting on a show for his benefit.

"We *are* friendly. Just wait till we're outside."

As soon as they had left the cool auditorium and were outside on the hot front porch of the school, Susan said, "All right, we're outside."

"It's my plot that I told you about. The idea is this: We'll go out to the university and play some of the music. And then we'll decide to go get something to eat."

"The only thing they have at this time of day is machines with candy bars."

"All right, we'll be dying for candy bars. And we'll go away and leave the violins there where we've been practicing—unguarded."

Susan gasped. "But you know somebody is after your aunt's violin. If they see us leave the instruments, they'll steal it."

"That's just the point. I won't go for the candy. I'll just pretend to. I'll let you go on and I'll stay behind and watch. And I'll see who it is—and nab him."

"Or her. But Bax, what if they're too quick? What if they really get it?"

"But they won't," he said triumphantly. "That's the

107

good luck about your not having the viola today. What we will do is to switch the violins in the cases."

Her face lit up. "So when the thief takes the fancy case, he gets my soggy fiddle. Oh Bax, don't nab him. Let him take it. Then I can buy a viola with the insurance money."

A kind of warning bell began to ring in the back of Bax's mind, saying some word he did not want to hear.

He stood silent a minute, half trying to hear the word and half trying to shut it out. The afternoon was quiet. He heard a car door slam as the last symphony people were leaving.

Then he heard something else. He clutched Susan's arm. "Did you hear that?"

"I hear sparrows chattering. They're always around."

"It sounded like someone moving, someone coughing. In the oleander bushes. Right here below where we're standing."

He moved cautiously to the porch railing and looked over. But the oleanders were too thick to see through. They were planted all along the foundation of the building, all the way to the corner on both sides.

"Sparrows," said Susan. "They're always in oleanders. Let's move before we melt down to grease in this heat."

They moved to the bus stop, where the bench was too hot to sit on. The bus was hot too. Bax craned his neck, trying to see who might be on the bus with them, or following in a car, but he saw no one who looked familiar or suspicious.

When they got out at the university stop, the sun was making all the new white buildings of the campus shimmer like mirages.

"They haven't even built Music yet." Susan set off at a fast stride, giving him a guided tour. "This big circular building is the general library. There's Administration, where my mother works. Now, here's the music library."

"That?" He stared at a long white trailer. He had heard his mother complain about having to give her piano classes in a lecture hall with poor acoustics, but this building was even less impressive. It was a mobile home unit like the one he lived in.

"Mother says the legislature wants to see Science all built up before they'll appropriate anything much for Arts."

Bax pointed at a row of garages, stretching down the hill toward a wide gulch full of tangled mesquite and dry brush. "What are those?" Sounds reached him—a soprano voice swooping up and down as if something terrifying were after it, a trumpeter triple-tonguing, a pianist pounding scales.

"Those are the practice cubicles. That's where you and I will be playing, as soon as we check out some music."

He followed her into the library trailer, his heart beating fast. The setup was ideal for his plot. If anybody wanted to follow and hide, the mesquite in the gulch made a great place to hide in. When it would come time for Bax himself to hide and watch, he could walk away with Susan as far as the trailer and then peer through from underneath it. There was no foundation skirting around the trailer, so he could see straight through to the doors of the practice cubicles.

The music librarian was a young woman with glasses and long hair. She knew Susan.

Bax hung back while Susan acted important.

"I want to check out some Beethoven music on my special card, the one my mother got for me."

"Which Beethoven music did you want? We have shelves and shelves of Beethoven."

"Orchestra music. This is my friend Sebastian Barlow. He plays in the Los Arboles Symphony, same as I do. He plays the violin." She said *violin* loudly, as if she wanted it to carry out through the closed windows and all over the campus.

"Hello, Sebastian. What orchestra music is on your mind? We have the big scores, with the orchestra parts, and we have the miniature scores, condensed down to book size."

Bax wanted to get out of there and get on with the plot. "We'll take both."

"Both of what?"

What had Mr. Hageman suggested? "*Egmont.*"

She switched on the lights of a long room full of shelves of music. "Third section. Bottom row."

He bumped his violin against the shelves as he made his way back to the third section. He could hear Susan continuing her speech, planting hints, overdoing it.

"Bax and I will probably get hungry later. Could we leave our instruments and go out for candy bars?"

He found the *Egmont* scores and pulled them out as he heard the librarian warn, "Not bright, that. Never leave anything anywhere. You never know who's snooping for something to hock."

Bax brought the scores of music to the counter. "Here's what we want. Got your card, Susan?"

"Of course I've got my card. It's the only one of its kind."

They came out from the cold air of the library trailer into the broiling heat of the pathway down to the practice cubicles.

"We'll take the very last one," Bax decided, "next to the gulch."

Susan nodded vigorously. "Then we'll practice music for a while," she fairly shouted. "Until we get hungry."

"Okay, okay. You've laid it on thick enough."

"I'm only trying to be helpful. You wanted me to help. You couldn't pull this off at all without me."

"I know that." They passed the sound of the shrill soprano voice, the trumpet, the piano scales. "Here, this is the one."

Inside the cubicle there was an upright piano, three bent music stands, a couple of rickety chairs. There was an electric heater on the floor for winter months and an air conditioning unit in the window for the summer session. The heat was unbearable.

Bax switched on the air conditioner. "Now for some *Egmont,* if we can make the music stay up on these stands."

They managed, but it wasn't easy. The music

wasn't easy to play, either. The print was crowded on the page, difficult for sight reading. They both kept playing wrong notes and getting lost, but they kept at it until Bax felt they had put on a good enough show of actually practicing.

"Game called," he announced at last. "I think that should do it."

Susan raised her voice. "Let's go get some *candy bars*. They're at the Student Union. You can't even *see* it from here."

Bax kept his voice low. "Now let's switch the violins in the cases. If we kneel down here with our backs to the window, nobody peering in can see what we're up to."

"They can't see much anyway," Susan giggled. "The window is so dirty."

Quickly they put the fine violin in Susan's battered pasteboard case and laid her ordinary fiddle in the splendid purple velvet. Bax pulled on the denim cover and pinched the snaps shut.

He straightened up and raised his voice. "I would sure like to take you up on that idea of getting candy bars, Susan. Show me the way." He thought he sounded hearty and sincere.

"I'll be *glad* to show you the way. It's out of *sight* from *here*."

He wished she wouldn't sound so stagy and phony. Anybody listening to her would get suspicious just from her tone of voice. If they really came into the cubicle with the idea of snatching his aunt's violin, they might take the precaution of checking out which violin was in which case.

Susan opened the door. "Let's *both* go to the Student *Union,*" she cried as if she were rallying an army to charge up a hill.

"I'm coming, I'm coming." He closed the door with a bang.

Their feet rasped noisily on the gravel of the path. He dragged his feet to make the scraping even louder, to announce that they were on their way.

"I'll hide here behind the library trailer and watch," he whispered.

"Can't I watch too?"

"One watcher is plenty."

"You're afraid I'll talk or jump around or something and scare the thief away."

She was exasperating. "You might. Go on, Susan."

"Oh, all right." She marched on over the rise toward the gym with her nose in the air.

Bax turned to peer under the trailer—and his heart seemed to leap into his throat. The plot worked! The door of the cubicle stood open—and someone came out!

All Bax could see was the scissor action of a pair of legs in black trousers, sprinting toward the mesquite thicket.

Bax raced around the corner of the trailer and rushed down the hill. Maybe he could find out who it was. He ran to the thicket and crashed inward a few feet, then stood still. He could see no one. There was not a sound, except for the shrieks and thumps of music practice.

He disentangled himself from scratching branches, and hurried to the cubicle.

There on the floor lay the denim-covered case, unopened, untouched.

The thief had taken the wrong one.

Whoever it was had vanished with Susan's old case—with his aunt's fine violin.

CHAPTER

20

Susan came charging in with candy bars. "Did it work, Bax?"

He felt paralyzed, staring at his terrible mistake. "It worked all wrong." His voice sounded strangled.

Susan fell to her knees before the violin case. "He was supposed to take this one," she wailed. "With my old fiddle. Now we can't get the insurance money for me to buy a viola."

He groaned. "We couldn't have anyhow, Susan. There's a word that's been bothering me, and it just hit me what it is. Fraud! That's the word. What we were doing was attempted fraud. There wouldn't have been any payoff on that."

She slowly unwrapped a candy bar. "But at least

115

you saw who it was. You did see the thief—didn't you?"

"Black trousers." He sat heavily on one of the chairs. "That was all I saw."

"I have some black jeans myself," said Susan. "So we can't even know if it was a he or a she. Want a candy bar?"

"I don't want anything. I want to crawl under something and starve to death. Susan, what am I going to do?"

She sat a minute, eating. "I'll tell you what, you can have my violin. Paste something on the tailpiece to look like a fleur-de-lis. Maybe nobody will notice."

"My aunt will notice. She's coming for the concert." He watched her finish her candy bar. "What will your mother say when you don't have your violin?"

"Nothing. She won't notice. May I eat your candy bar?"

He nodded. The sight of the candy, the sight of the violin case, the sight of the whole visible world made him sick.

Susan peeled paper. "My mother is so used to me bringing the school viola home and leaving my violin at school. Or leaving them both at school. She doesn't pay any attention."

"My mother pays attention." And his father had never got the sales slip from Aunt Daphne.

"Let's take the music back to the librarian and ask her if she saw anybody around," suggested Susan.

"She couldn't have. The person dodged in from the bushes behind the building here and then dodged right back there again."

"Did you look?"

"I looked." He showed her his arms and legs. "That's where I got all these scratches."

"So the thief got scratched too. Now we have to put out a dragnet for a person with scratches—"

Bax shook his head. "There must be ways to wriggle through that brush. The person had plenty of time to look around while we were practicing and figure out his escape route."

"Or hers."

Bax got up heavily and shut off the air conditioner. In the sudden quiet, Susan's candy wrapper crackled noisily above the muffled sound of piano scales. "Well, let's go. I guess I'll take you up on that offer of your violin, Susan. It'll tide me through till I can think of something."

But all week he couldn't think of anything.

He trudged through the hot bright days wrapped in his own personal cold gray fog.

He had to force himself to eat, under his mother's watchful eyes. He slept poorly but tried to put on a normal healthy act.

He pasted a little white paper in the shape of a fleur-de-lis on the tailpiece of Susan's violin, and practiced with his mute on, so that the difference in tone couldn't be noticed. As long as he stayed back in his room with the violin, he got away with it. But he knew he wasn't going to get away with it when his aunt arrived on the scene. He wasn't even going to get away with it when old Mr. Per Se took a look.

And he couldn't get away with it inside himself.

Even if his parents didn't know what had happened, he knew.

The time came when his parents had to know too.

It was the night before the final rehearsal. Bax had tried to eat supper, but he had not succeeded very well.

The phone rang. Formerly he would have made a dive for it, but tonight he only ambled back toward his room.

His mother called, "It's for you."

Bax took the phone with its twenty-foot cord into his parents' bedroom and shut the door.

It was Susan. "Bax, I've got bad news."

"Doesn't matter," Bax said dully. "You can't make things worse."

"Yes, I can. I have to have my violin for rehearsal tomorrow."

His heart, already heavy as a lead weight, grew even heavier. "But why?"

"There was a big storm in the mountains, up around Wagon Pass. The music camp is cut off till the roads are cleared."

"You mean the junior high orchestra director—"

"Is stuck. They got word out by ham radio. Nobody's hurt, but everybody's stuck."

Bax's private gray fog turned to black cloud. "And the school viola is up there, stuck with him."

"Oh Bax, if I could pretend to be sick, I'd stay home from rehearsal. But I'm healthy as a horse."

"If I could pretend to be dead—" said Bax bitterly.

After they hung up, he dragged the phone back to the living room. Both of his parents were sitting on the sofa, not talking, not reading, just sitting.

They looked like a jury. It was showdown time.

"Sit over there, son." His father waved toward the piano bench. "Now tell us. Why have you been behaving like a ghost all week? A brave ghost, I'll grant you. We could see the effort you've put into your attempt to act normal and cheerful. We assume that you are trying to shield us from something, which is commendable. But perhaps we can help."

"Help?" Bax choked. The only helpful thing they could do would be to commit him to some place far away, deep and dark. "Aunt Daphne's violin is gone."

His mother clutched her throat. "But then whose—"

"I borrowed Susan's. She was in on the plot. But it was my plot."

His father struck his fist on the sofa arm. "She never sent that bill of sale. She probably doesn't have it. She is so scatterbrained—always was."

At least she had a brain to scatter, Bax thought darkly. He had no brain at all. "It wouldn't do any good if she had. You couldn't collect insurance."

"Why not?"

"Because this was a case of attempted fraud."

His father frowned. "Who attempted fraud?"

"I did."

There was nothing to do but tell the whole miserable story, and wait for the ax to fall.

His father's ax fell first on Aunt Daphne. "Of all the idiot ideas for that woman to have—to foist a dangerous instrument on a mere child."

His mother said, "Now, Charles."

His father got up and paced. "I know, I know,

that's how Daphne is, has been, and always will be. But what about you, Bax? Were you planning to use your friend's violin in this grand concert for which I see posters plastered all over town?"

"I wasn't planning anything. I didn't know what to do. Anyhow, I can't use the violin. Susan has to have it herself."

His mother said, "Daphne will be bringing his violin back with her. He can play that for the concert."

But his father squashed that. "Our son admits to a crime of attempted fraud. This should not go unpunished. I think that a just punishment will be for him not to participate in the concert at all."

The concert—for which everything had been building up for so long—the event toward which they had all been aiming, all summer! Like life flashing before a drowning man, Bax saw again the newspaper story announcing formation of the orchestra, the sign on the hotel's showroom door announcing that auditions were being held inside. It all seemed so long ago. And it hurt.

He felt as though knives were twisting in his stomach. It was a punishment, for sure. And he had to admit it was just.

He got up painfully. "I'll call Susan and tell her she can come get her violin."

But his father wasn't finished yet. "No, you will take the violin to her personally. When is the next rehearsal?"

"Tomorrow."

"You will take it to the rehearsal hall and hand it over to her there."

Inside his head Bax could hear the exciting medley of the sounds of tuning. He could see the eager agitated orchestra members bracing to play. And he could see himself, plodding despondently up to Susan in the viola section, handing her the violin, enduring while she screeched a lot of dramatic commiserations and made him feel worse.

This was going to be just about the hardest thing he had ever done.

CHAPTER 21

Next day, Bax strapped Susan's violin onto the handlebar of his bicycle. The weather was strangely threatening. Wind buffeted from all sides, with no prevailing direction. Dark clouds piled high above the mountains that ringed Los Arboles Valley.

He headed for Arroyo High. Sand lifted from vacant lots and spun in the air. It stung at his eyes and gritted in his teeth.

He pedaled as slowly as he could, trying to postpone the pain of confrontation. But it seemed like only minutes before Arroyo High loomed up in front of him.

To make it worse, he was early. The first cars with musicians were just arriving.

He chained his bike to the bike rack and went into the auditorium, taking his time.

The stage was all set up in the familiar semicircle of chairs and stands. He sat in the darkened auditorium, swallowing past the lump in his throat. Only a few people were in position as yet. The tympanist was tuning. A bass viol growled.

Bax took one look at his own chair, there in the back row—empty, of course—and at the space underneath it where he had always stashed the violin case. Empty. He shut his eyes.

Scrapings and tootlings and the murmur of voices increased until it sounded as though most of the orchestra was present. Then he heard a high chatter and laugh that could only belong to Susan.

Opening his eyes, he pulled himself out of the seat, and made his way up the narrow stairs onto the stage, back behind the cello section, toward the violas.

He was stopped by Mr. Bolden. "Young man, it came to my attention that you were not doing anything about those program notes."

Knives twisted in his stomach again. Guilty as charged. He had not been doing anything about anything lately. He mumbled evasively, "I didn't really know what was wanted."

"So I took matters into my own hands. I wrote the program notes myself."

Beyond Mr. Bolden, Susan was hopping up and down, waving her arms toward Bax. His irritation increased—why must she call so much attention to herself—and to him?

He tried to edge past Mr. Bolden. "That's fine, sir."

"I'm sure you will be wanting to get into place and

tune your instrument. Are you enjoying the use of that instrument?"

Mr. Bolden stared at the denim-covered case with that old look of greed.

Bax could only stammer, "Well—I can't exactly—"

"You remember what I told you when I first saw it. That may be a very valuable instrument."

Susan's voice caroled high. "Bax! Sebastian! Hurry up, Mr. Hageman's coming already."

"Your friend seems to be calling you," said Mr. Bolden. "Don't let me stand in your way."

He continued to stand squarely in Bax's way, but Bax managed to shove past him.

"Here's your fiddle, Susan." He thrust the case at her.

"Oh Bax, isn't it marvelous?"

"Nothing's marvelous." He turned to go.

"About your violin," she burbled on. "Your aunt's violin. Being back."

Had she gone crazy? "Back of what?"

"Back here. Under your chair."

"It is not. I looked."

"It is. I looked. I'm taller than you and I can see farther and it's there. Get over there and see for yourself. And hurry up. There's Mr. Hageman jumping on the podium to start."

Amid the deafening din, Bax snaked his way among stands and instruments across to the other side of the orchestra. He pulled up beside his own chair, almost afraid to look. But he did look. And there was Susan's battered violin case under his chair!

With trembling legs, he sat down on the chair and reached under for the case.

Mr. Hageman let out his whistle. Bax pulled at the case. It wouldn't budge. Something was holding it tight.

Mr. Hageman said "Tune."

The oboe's A spun out. Holding tight to his end of the case, Bax leaned all the way down and looked under the seat of his chair. A hand was reaching out from under the curtain, gripping the violin case! He could see just a flick of white shirt cuff, black coat sleeve.

Bax grabbed with both hands and yanked. The other hand let go. Bax tumbled forward, bumping into the chair in front of him.

Behind him the curtains billowed in a swish of air as a door slammed. Whoever it was, the person had escaped—had run out through the stage door.

Mr. Hageman's voice barked. "Sebastian! What are you doing standing on your head? Yoga exercises? Straighten up and tune."

Bax hastily righted himself and opened the case. There lay Aunt Daphne's violin, unharmed, the fleur-de-lis shining mother-of-pearl pink. Where had it been? And why was it back? And who had been trying to drag it away again?

One thing he made up his mind about, for sure. He was going to haul the violin out to Mr. Rucci for an appraisal, right after rehearsal.

Susan came surging over to him at the break, holding the fine case high above everyone's head.

"Is it okay, Bax? Nothing happened to it?"

"Not a thing. It's as good as ever."

"Well, here's the fancy case. Hand me mine."

Bax's stand partner was watching the transaction with close attention. "May I inquire the reason for this exchange of containers?"

"My violin got stolen. My aunt's, I mean. And then it got returned."

"And why would someone do that?"

Bax looked at him sharply. He certainly was interested. "Maybe they're just crazy."

Susan had a theory. "Maybe they found out it's really a terribly valuable old Del Fiore, and they couldn't hock it or sell it or anything, because it would be spotted. You know, like when people steal some super-famous painting out of a museum and it's so well known, they finally can't do anything with it but put it back."

Bax gazed at the violin. "I'm going to find out about that," he announced. "Right after rehearsal, I'm going to take it out to Mr. Rucci and get an appraisal."

"You're going on your bike?" asked Susan. "In this weird weather? It may storm."

"I'll just have to go fast and beat out the storm," Bax said. "My aunt is landing at the airport this very minute. My mother is meeting her and telling her I've lost the violin. So when I come back and show her that I have it—and show my father that I did something about the insurance business—I can finally hold my head up in my own family."

Susan giggled. "Are you giving up your life of crime? No more fraud schemes?"

"I'm going straight," he promised wryly. "I have seen the light."

126

"I'll see you at Kip's fish fry."

He wanted to bolt immediately after rehearsal, but Mr. Hageman issued one of his "Sebastian, see me" commands.

Bax hurried to the podium. "Mr. Hageman, I'm sorry I didn't do better about those program notes, but Mr. Bolden says he took care of them. I have to go, sir."

"Where to?"

"Out to Mr. Rucci. I want him to look over this violin."

Mr. Hageman turned pale. "You are going to have a professional examination—"

Impatiently Bax explained. "So I can report to my aunt. She's at my house right now. She flew down here so she can come to the concert tomorrow. I have to go, sir. The weather is funny today and I want to hurry."

Mr. Hageman had now turned pink. "Yes—yes, certainly. Go."

It was a long, very slightly uphill pull toward Rancho Vista, the sparsely settled area where Mr. Rucci had his place. The rise was small but steady. Bax felt it in his leg muscles more than he actually saw it, till he paused to catch his breath and turned to look back.

The clouds were rolling in across the valley now. The wind was hot, buffeting him, making the bike hard to control. It tore great balloons of tumbleweed loose and sent them sailing.

A meandering shortcut led downhill among the clumps of grease-bush. Bax resolved to use that path for his return trip. It seemed to go in the general direction of home.

He squinted suddenly. Something moved along that path. Or did it? Did someone dodge behind a grease-bush and stay there, motionless?

Sand swirled, obscuring his vision. Prickles of fear rippled up his spine. Was someone following him?

There were a few houses scattered along the road, some dilapidated outbuildings, parked trucks, abandoned cars. As he went on, he kept trying to look back, but he could not catch sight of anyone following. It took most of his attention to hold the bike on the road in the teeth of the changeable wind.

Mr. Rucci's shop was set well back from the road. It looked more like a barn than a violin shop. As Bax approached, he figured out that it must have been a real barn years ago, when somebody tried ranching on this arid soil.

He skidded swiftly to a stop by the big double door. He looked back, down the rutted driveway and along the road. Branches of huge old cottonwood trees flopped in the wind. Tumbleweed rolled low, rode high. It was no use to try to see anyone. There were so many places to hide.

He leaned the bike against the side of the building and did not fasten the padlock. He might want to make a fast getaway.

There was a smaller door, cut into the big double door. The doorknob rasped as he turned it. The hinges squeaked. Bax stepped into darkness. The floorboards creaked. Strange shapes crouched in the gloom. "Hello?" His voice sounded hollow and scared. "Is anybody here?"

"Oh, excuse, excuse." The cry came from the far corner. "I was only taking a small nap. I will turn on the light."

An overhead bulb sprang to light, flooding the enormous cluttered room with a hard glare.

And there in person stood the devil.

CHAPTER
22

The man's hair stuck out in all directions. He wore a black coat, a white shirt with starched collar, a flowing black tie. His shoulders hunched high. His arms hung, long and angular.

Bax fell back a pace, bumping against a rack of guitar parts. "Are you Mr. Rucci?"

The man's eyes glittered. "This is the shop of Signor Rucci, violinmaker, mender, and appraiser." He leaned across the counter, which was strewn with violin pegs, strings, cakes of rosin, bridges, pots of glue. "I am here behind the counter of the shop. Why should you have to ask whether I am who I am?"

Bax knew it was not polite to make remarks about how anybody looked, but he could not help blurting it out. "Did anybody ever tell you that you look like old pictures of Niccolò Paganini?"

How was he going to take that?

He took it by cackling happily. "Yes, many people have pointed it out. So it entertains me to play up to the resemblance. I dress the part, as you see."

Nobody else in Los Arboles would wear an outfit like that outside of a stage show. Black trousers. The legs Bax had seen running with the violin from the practice cubicle had been wearing black. Could they have been Mr. Rucci's legs?

Mr. Rucci went on talking, growling to himself. "I want to emphasize that my chief concern is violins. University students keep bringing me guitars to repair. Miserable guitars!" He swept his arm in a wide contemptuous gesture, hitting against a guitar that hung from a rafter and setting it swinging.

Violins in various stages of construction occupied shelves. A couple of cellos lay on their sides. A bass viol leaned up against a partition that must formerly have been a horse stall. And guitars, guitars were everywhere.

Wind rattled the door. Mr. Rucci's glittering stare rested on Bax. "Surely, my boy, you did not travel out here in the teeth of a windstorm to comment on the peculiarity of my appearance."

Bax stepped firmly forward and lifted the violin case. "I want an appraisal on the value of—"

With a sweep of his arm, Mr. Rucci cleared the counter, knocking everything to the floor. He pounced with a piercing cry. "You brought that violin! And about time, too."

Bax held onto it. "About time for what?"

"I have been trying to get my hands on that violin for weeks. To examine it for my client."

"What client?" Bax demanded boldly.

"Silence, my boy." Mr. Rucci put a bony finger to his lips and glanced warily toward the door, then toward the grimy window. Bax glanced at the window too—and could almost have sworn that he saw a face suddenly withdraw! It was only a split second. He could not even tell whether the face had a beard—if there really was a face there at all.

"My client," said Mr. Rucci in a hoarse whisper, "is known to me only as Signor Ignoto. He does not want his real identity known."

"Why not?"

"Because he has so much money."

Most people with money wanted to put on a display. "I don't get it."

Mr. Rucci leaned across the violin case, eyeball to eyeball. "Signor Ignoto is a collector of a variety of works of art. He has agents in many fields looking for valuable items for him, and we mail our communications to his post office box. But if it became known to the sellers that he is interested, they would immediately raise their price."

Bax's mind popped an idea. "I'll bet I know who it is. I'll bet it's Mr. Hector Bolden."

"Hush hush hush." Mr. Rucci waved his long arms frantically. "Of course it is. But he would not employ me as an agent if I told anybody."

"I only want to know the value of the violin for insurance," said Bax. "It belongs to my aunt, and it isn't for sale."

Mr. Rucci's bony fingers unsnapped the denim cover and opened the case. "My boy, you are no doubt aware that this instrument has the marking of a Del Fiore."

"I know."

"I assure you then, if this is a real Del Fiore, and my client wants to buy it, it will be for sale. However—"

Lifting the violin as though it were a precious piece of porcelain, Mr. Rucci held it up under the light, squinting in through the F-holes to look at the label inside. Then he turned it over, examining the back. He ran his thumb along the edge of the top.

Bax asked breathlessly, "However, what?"

Mr. Rucci dropped the violin back into the case with an unceremonious clunk. "However," he said flatly, "if your aunt decides to try to sell this instrument, she will be lucky to get four hundred dollars."

The wind raised a moan around the creaky building.

"So it's not a Del Fiore at all?"

"It is not even a very good imitation. I see violins like this by the hundreds. In the latter nineteenth century, German factories turned them out. Imitation Stradivarius. Imitation Stainer. Phony markings, phony labels. Signor Ignoto will have no further interest."

But somebody had an interest. Somebody had been interested enough to steal it. If the violin had no great value, why were they so interested?

Mr. Rucci went on. "I shall have to keep it for a time, to make out a complete description and report for my client, as well as a detailed analysis and appraisal for your aunt."

"But I need it tomorrow afternoon for the concert," cried Bax in alarm. "Why can't you do it now?"

A flash of lightning lit the room starkly. "Because my home is up the hill, and I want to get there before this storm descends on us. And because you need to hurry along home too. And because you shouldn't be carrying any violin around in a storm. This one will be safe in my locked vault. You can come for it in the morning."

Bax's mind was beginning to churn up a new idea. The thief had taken the violin—and then returned it. So the thief had found out the same thing Mr. Rucci just reported—that the violin wasn't of any special value.

But suppose the thief was wrong in believing it was the violin that mattered. Suppose there was something particularly valuable about—the case?

Bax said, "You can lock up the violin. But I'd like to take the case home."

"Empty? That is a peculiar idea."

Bax snapped the cover on. "It may be a peculiar case. I want to examine it."

Mr. Rucci hurried to carry the violin to a vault built into one of the old horse stalls. He locked the vault, turned out the light, and fairly ran to the door, with Bax bumping behind him in the darkness.

Mr. Rucci turned the doorknob and the door swung inward. The blast of sandy wind knocked them both back against the wall.

They pushed out into the wild wind. Mr. Rucci grabbed the knob, trying to pull the door of the shop shut. Bax had to help him pull, with all his might, until they finally got the door closed so that it could be locked.

Without a word, Mr. Rucci headed up the hill.

The wind had blown the bike over. Bax picked it up and started to strap the violin case onto the handlebar—then stopped cold.

Someone was coming around the corner of the barn, straight toward him.

CHAPTER 23

He jumped on the bike and started wobbling down the bumpy driveway as fast as he could go. Turning into the road and pedaling as hard as he could, he saw a strange sight ahead of him, spread over the valley. It was a solid wall of gray. It looked like the edge of a sandstorm—but not like the sand he had often seen. A sandstorm was a kind of boiling dirty tan color. This was solid silver, and moving toward him.

Rain!

The first big drops started splattering on him as he was almost at the turnoff for the shortcut. Stopping a moment, he looked back. There was a man, running! Bax caught sight of him just before a sheet of rain swallowed him up. He wore jeans and a blue shirt—and he had no beard.

That man must want the violin—which Bax didn't have. No storm was going to stop him. What would he do if he actually caught up and found out the case was empty? Suddenly Bax felt scared. What had he laid himself open to?

He felt terribly awkward, holding the handle of the violin case and the grip of the bike at the same time. But he had to keep moving. He swung into the shortcut path. Maybe the rain screened him enough that the pursuer would not see him turn.

He was drenched. The cover of the violin case was soaked.

The path rapidly became a slippery running brook. The cascade of drops pelted and splashed on frothy puddles.

His tires skidded dangerously. Cactus seemed to reach to clutch the spokes of his wheels. Low grease-bush branches scratched skin off his bare legs.

For a while he was too busy to dare to look back. Then he ventured it. Rain gusted before his eyes, obscuring everything. His front wheel struck a boulder, and he had to concentrate all his strength on righting it.

His breath was coming hard. He glanced back again. The man was there, far behind him but coming along, slipping, falling, getting up again.

Bax panted hoarsely, pumping his legs. If he could just make it down to Spanish Trail Highway, he would be almost home. The highway would be a flowing river, since the ditching and drainage piping still weren't finished along there—but surely a bicycle could plow through a river faster than a man on foot.

Suddenly the front wheel hit against another boulder. It slued him sideways. The rear wheel was thrown right into the branches of a large strong grease-bush. The branches seemed to clutch the spokes and hold on. Bax put the violin case down in the mud, and hauled and yanked at the bike. But the tough branches were tangled in the chain, rammed into the sprocket. He had to abandon the bike.

He grabbed up the violin case and floundered on. Now he had no advantage over his pursuer: they were both on foot.

He dared to look back, between whipping gusts of rain. The man had come upon the bicycle now. He was wiping water from his eyes, gazing around with jerky motions, here and there, as if trying to locate which way Bax had gone.

Bax dove behind a grease-bush and crouched there. A small rise was ahead of him. If he could slither over that rise unseen, the man would not be able to observe which way he had gone.

He chanced it—plunging up and over. And he smacked right into a yellow wall.

But it wasn't a wall. It was a piece of heavy road-working equipment. He was almost at the highway!

Very soon, his pursuer would probably climb the rise too, and look around. If there were only some place he could hide!

He looked up at the yellow rig he had run against. There was a driver's cab up there, covered over—a good place to be protected from the rain, but certainly no place to hide. If he climbed up there, he would be trapped.

Frantically he looked around. He pushed his way

around the machine, feet slipping and sinking in the oozing mud.

Great concrete pipes lay in an irregular row. Mounds of wet gravel were piled around them or had slid against them in miniature landslides.

A pipe—that would be big enough for him to hide in.

He took a plunge toward the nearest pipe. It was big enough for a person his size to fit into, even to sit up in. He dropped to his knees and scrambled in.

It was dark in the pipe. The far end of it was almost closed by a slide of mud. Water trickled through like a brooklet. He sat on gravel, smelling the wet cement, hearing the pounding of the rain overhead.

Then a cold thought hit him. What if the pursuer had watched through Mr. Rucci's window—and knew all along that Bax did not have the violin? If that were true, then what the pursuer was after really *was* the case!

Whoever took the violin from the practice cubicle had not wanted the case. But someone was out there in the rain right now, with a different idea.

Bax clawed at the cover of the case. What could there be about the case that mattered so much?

It was soaking wet now. He ran his hands over the top of the case. Then he turned it over. The bottom was of different material than the top, he already knew. Now he found it was of very inferior material. It was not real leather, but an imitation that was peeling loose around the edges.

The sounds outside and overhead changed, diminished. The rain was letting up.

He sat rigid, listening. He heard a banging noise,

against metal. The man must be thumping around the yellow machine.

Bax tore at the covering of the bottom of the case. If there was any mysterious concealment in that case, he had to know, fast.

He heard a man's voice. The sound came muffled into his hiding place. "Is someone up there? Hey there!" Then scrambling of feet. The man must be climbing up to see if Bax had tried to hide in the cab.

Feverishly he ripped, then felt over the bare wooden bottom of the case.

There was a square cut out of the wood! And inside that square was a slick little pouch, like an envelope made of oilcloth. A waterproof pouch, hidden in the case, covered over—it had to be something smuggled. Something valuable, something terribly important.

Crouching in the dim light, he could hear the sounds outside, the man's feet slogging around. He crept to the farthest end of the pipe, where it was darkest. Surely the man would not think of looking in here. If he did, he really could not see anything.

But with the unpredictability of desert storms, the clouds in the west suddenly lifted. The sun was almost down. A ray of sun shafted straight into the pipe.

At that moment, the legs of the man appeared at the opening. Bax saw something gleam, something bright sewn onto the trousers below the knees. Horrified, he held his breath. Was the man going to bend down and look in?

He did. And he cried hoarsely, "There you are. That case—I must have that case."

Bax thrust the small pouch into the front of his T-shirt as the man bent down to crawl in. He abandoned the case and started digging madly with both hands, delving at the mud wall in front of him.

The man was crawling on hands and knees toward him—reaching for him.

With a final effort, Bax cleared enough of the gravel to make room to escape.

The man grabbed at his foot. He got hold of it. Bax assaulted the opening. With a violent wrench, he yanked his foot free and climbed out into the air.

He paused just for a second, to give one fast kick, pushing gravel back into the opening. Then he took off running.

With the sunset illuminating the dripping landscape, he knew where he was. He was headed for the tamarack trees that rimmed Cactus Acres Trailer Park.

He climbed over a fence, cut through yards, dodged along winding ways that he knew well from chases after his dog Stub, and pulled up, panting, at his own home.

There was a car parked out front—Mr. Hageman's.

He didn't dare to go in the front, muddy as he was. He rushed around to the back, and into the service area.

"Mother! Dad! Everybody! I've got something. I've got whatever the mystery of the violin is all about."

He grabbed for the nearest towel and dried his hands, then reached inside his shirt for the little pouch he had found. Maybe there were thousands of dollars in there. Maybe there were jewels.

Aunt Daphne appeared in the doorway. "Nephew

Sebastian. You look perfectly dreadful. Where is my violin?"

His mother crowded beside her. "Good heavens."

His father and Mr. Hageman joined them.

"Your violin is all right," Bax panted. "But the case came to pieces. And this—these—"

With great care, he opened the little pouch, and took out some pieces of paper. They were brownish with age, about seven inches by five. Strange scratchings were on them, in ink, words he couldn't read.

But he knew what they were!

Mr. Hageman spoke, sounding as unbelieving as if he were seeing a ghost. "Sebastian, do you realize what you have there?"

Bax spread the papers reverently on top of the dryer. "The missing pages of the Beethoven Notebooks."

CHAPTER

24

Bax hurried through a shower and a change of clothes. "I have to get over to Kip's."

Mr. Hageman offered, "May I drive you there?"

"I'm coming along, too," said Aunt Daphne. "You have a lot of explaining to do, Emmet."

The three of them climbed into the front seat of the car, and Mr. Hageman started his explaining. "It all began with a friend of mine, Gary McGill, who is in our government's intelligence service—"

"A spy!" cried Bax.

Mr. Hageman steered through swirling brown water, onto the highway. "He called me one day while I was in Munich, doing music research. They had cracked down on a smuggling ring that dealt in all kinds of things—jewelry, documents, musical instruments. One violin had been traced to a little shop—"

"Where I bought it," Aunt Daphne exclaimed.

"You bought it just one minute ahead of me. McGill wanted me to look it over, but you were just coming out with it. But then you turned up with it on shipboard."

"And you wanted to examine it." Aunt Daphne did not sound very pleased. "Was it you who came sneaking into my stateroom?"

"It was. And I was afraid you recognized me. That's why I avoided you after that."

"Cut me dead, was what you did."

Bax demanded, "Was it you who came snooping here that first night? Was it you I chased?" A shudder swept through him. Who had chased *him*, today?

"It was. By then I was beginning to hope Daphne hadn't recognized me after all. So I followed her, to find out her next move."

"To Los Angeles. With the wrong violin." He was almost afraid to ask the next question. "Is that why you let me into the orchestra? Only because I had that violin and you wanted to keep an eye on it?"

"Certainly not." The car nearly went out of control on the gravel-strewn pavement, and Mr. Hageman righted it with a jerk. "I would never lower the quality of my orchestra by admitting any player of insufficient ability. I fully expect you to be among the first stands by the time you are a senior in high school."

Bax felt as if he were swelling up like a balloon.

But there were enough frightening unknowns in the story to keep him down to earth. "In the stateroom.

In the trailer park," he said thoughtfully. Something bothered him. At last he put his finger on it. "Hair. What about that mad mane of hair?"

"A wig."

Bax lurched forward, nearly bumping his head on the windshield. "That's it!"

"What's what?"

"A wig! Phony hair! That must be what Half-face had on when he came to rehearsal." His voice rose high with excitement. "Phony hair—a beard. And he didn't have it on today. But he had on the embroidered jeans. Turn right."

Mr. Hageman swung the car to the right. "What for?"

"To visit Big Daddy. Straight ahead to that signal and then left."

"I hope you know what you're doing," Aunt Daphne said.

"I hope so too. I hope he's there. I hope he's not over in Cactus Acres trying to steal the notebook pages back."

Mr. Hageman read the sign on the house window. BIG DADDY'S PRACTICE PAD.

Lights blazed in the front room.

"Come on, let's go," cried Bax.

They tromped up onto the small porch. Thuds, twangs, wails of musical instruments were tangling inside.

Bax rang the bell and knocked on the door, but no one inside could have heard. "We'll just have to charge in."

"Lead on, Emmet," said Aunt Daphne.

They walked into a dark dining room and were enveloped in a solid cloud of deafening sound. None of the musicians in the living room even looked up. Mr. Hageman and Aunt Daphne stood fascinated, staring at the noisy group.

Bax figured that Half-face would not be a member of the grooving gang, as he remembered how the music had already been in full swing when he had come from the library. By himself, he ventured into the dark kitchen. It smelled of cheese and garlic. Something soft brushed his ankle and he jumped. But it was just a cat.

Suddenly the light flared on. A man in a black suit loomed up before him—leaped toward him—and seized him by the hair.

"Got you!" the man shouted.

The man tugged him toward the door.

"Help!" yelled Bax.

The music thundered on. Mr. Hageman and Aunt Daphne could not possibly hear him.

But the light and movement got their attention. They came to the doorway.

The man looked up and let go of Bax's hair. "Emmet!"

Mr. Hageman barked, "Gary McGill!"

Aunt Daphne raised her voice shrilly. "What is this, class reunion?"

They had to yell above the racket. Bax darted to the kitchen door and opened it. "Come on out where we can hear."

They came out into the warm darkness. The desert smelled of a hundred spices, as it always did after rain.

"What did you take from that violin case?" McGill demanded from Bax. "Papers? What kind of papers?"

Mr. Hageman said, "The Beethoven Notebook papers. We have them in a safe place. I thought you were in Germany, McGill. What are you doing here?"

McGill let out an explosive sigh of great relief. "Saving my life. Or saving my job, which amounts to the same thing. Saving our country's reputation among nations."

Aunt Daphne said indignantly, "By running boys down into drainage pipes?"

"I wasn't running a boy down, I was trying to unravel a smuggling plot. I'm sorry, kid, but you had what I was after. I apologize for trying to terrify you just now."

Aunt Daphne said sharply, "You could have asked politely for the stuff in the first place."

"No, I couldn't. Everything was top secret. The papers had been stolen—from my desk. The government did not want that known. Now the lid is off, and the whole story can be told."

Mr. Hageman put his hand on Bax's shoulder. "This young fellow has a supper date. Suppose you tell us about it on our way there."

McGill joined them in the car and talked all the way to Kip's place.

By the time he joined Susan and Kip at Kip's dinette table, Bax had the whole story together, and it was a hair raiser.

CHAPTER 25

"You're late," said Kip.

"But wait till you hear why." In the middle of the table there was a steaming platter of fish crisped in corn-meal, and it smelled marvelous. "You remember about those Beethoven Notebooks, Kip?"

Kip nodded. "Ceremony of restoring them to East Germany postponed. The Read-Everything Service never forgets."

"Let me clue you in on some history. After World War II, a double agent posed as a musicologist, and he stole all the Notebooks from the Eastern Zone and tried to sell them to the West."

"Have some fish." Susan didn't sound very thrilled by history.

"But his cover was blown," Bax went on, "and the Notebooks were confiscated and returned. All but a few."

Kip leaned forward. "And where are the few?"

"You won't believe this, but they're safe in my home in Cactus Acres."

Susan shrieked. "You found priceless papers? In that violin?"

"Not in the violin. In the case."

"Where is the case now?"

"In a drainpipe by the highway. Unless McGill has picked it up."

Kip asked, "Who's McGill?"

Bax gave them the rundown on McGill.

Susan looked at Bax with fascination. "Wow. Was he the one who took it from the university?"

"Remember when I thought I heard somebody in the oleanders while we were talking on the porch? He was the somebody. He had on black trousers that day because his jeans were in the wash."

"Now you're famous," cried Kip.

"I'm hungry," said Bax. He couldn't remember ever being so hungry in his life. Was it from the exertion of the chase through the desert? Whatever it was he ate enough fish for about two and a half people.

The next morning he wrestled his bike free of the clutching grease-bush, and went to Mr. Rucci for the violin.

He had a few more questions to ask—and he got the answers. Mr. Rucci had been the one who lurked in the curtains. He had been the one Bax chased around school to the basement steps.

As Mr. Rucci tucked the violin into Bax's old case for him, Bax asked, "And did you mess with the violin at the next break?"

"Not I. Your stand partner decided to play it for his own amusement. But I was the one who tried to pull it out from under your chair yesterday, after that other fellow sneaked in and put it there."

Bax grinned. "And I hung on."

"To my surprise. I had assumed you were not coming."

Bax ate a double-size lunch, and then came the ordeal of getting into his one presentable good suit. After living in loose sportswear, this felt like imprisonment. The suit seemed to have shrunk since the last time he wore it.

The Arroyo High School auditorium was filled to capacity. Bax's family was there, and Gary McGill was with them. Susan's mother sat in the front row. Kip sat in the back.

The familiar tuning sounds rumbled. Then— silence.

Mr. Hageman loped onto the stage, raised his baton, and signaled the long swelling single tone opening the Overture to *Coriolanus*. Then *Crack!* the big chord ripped forth with an electric thrill.

At the end of the first half of the concert, the applause roared the appreciation of the full house.

Before the second half, lights were dimmed. The orchestra sat silent. Mr. Bolden marched pompously to the podium.

"Ladies and gentlemen, in my research to prepare the program notes—" He went on about what a wonderful researcher he was, while Bax tried to pull his cuffs down. There seemed to be an unusual amount of wrist showing.

Mr. Bolden finally got to the Beethoven Notebooks and gave their history, all the way up to the theft of the papers from Mr. McGill's desk.

Then he got onto the subject of the violin, and the concealment of the papers in the case. "This very case," boomed Mr. Bolden, holding the mutilated case up for the audience to see.

Bax craned his neck, looking over the audience. McGill was out there somewhere. Surely he would come up and take a bow.

Mr. Bolden wound up, "And now I want you all to meet the person responsible for making this great discovery—I repeat, this great discovery. Come up and take a bow—Johann Sebastian Barlow."

Bax felt stunned. It was like walking in a dream, threading his way past orchestra players to the front of the stage.

The lights beamed on him, the applause welled up like thunder.

What a long time it seemed since the day he had come skulking in here wondering if he really belonged at all.

He turned to say, "Thank you, sir" to Mr. Bolden —and made another great discovery. He used to look straight at Mr. Bolden's chin. Now he looked straight at his nose.

At last, he had commenced the Growth Spurt.